Wolf's Capture

Kodiak Point, Book Five

Eve Langlais

Copyright © November 2014, Eve Langlais
Cover Art by Aubrey Rose © October 2014
Edited by Devin Govaere
Copy Edited by Amanda L. Pederick
Produced in Canada

Published by Eve Langlais
1606 Main Street, PO Box 151
Stittsville, Ontario, Canada, K2S1A3
http://www.EveLanglais.com

ISBN-13: 978-1503013940
ISBN-10: 1503013944

ALL RIGHTS RESERVED

𝔓rologue

Everyone dreaded the 'I told you so' moment. You knew which one she meant. *The event*—and, yes, she finger quoted as she said it. In retrospect it was quite easy to spot, as it was the catalyst that would forever alter the course of her life.

And it was totally my fault.

As Layla was dragged from her home, kicking and yelling, she couldn't help but flashback to her father's latest lecture—given just that morning. Before you jumped to the conclusion her father was a strict disciplinarian, she should note she fully deserved the boring speech considering he'd caught her, yet again, disobeying.

Act of defiance one hundred and sixty-one. He kept count.

"You must hide what you are, Layla. Hide it well because if anyone ever finds out, they'll come for you."

Blah. Blah. Blah. Nothing new here. She tuned out the rest of his speech, which went on for a while along that vein.

The gist of the rebuke was, "Don't use your power. Ever."

As in never.

Ever.

Which sucked.

Because really, how could she stifle it? Her skill, her super-special, top-secret ability was a part of who she was. It lived within her. Beckoned her. At times she could feel it as it pulsed just under her skin. Much like a treat, it tempted and cajoled her into tasting. *Just a nibble.* Or, in her case, a simple act. The barest thought and Poof! She could do incredible things. *Special* things.

The older she got, the harder she found it to restrain herself. And why should she?

I can't help who I am. A bird flies. A dog barks. My dad lectures. Why can't I just be me?

Once she hit those rebellious pre-teen years, she stopped fighting her innate power. She let it loose. Such a relief, and, once started, impossible to stop. She dabbled in the forbidden—and loved it.

Which in turn led to more experimenting.

If I can do this, then I wonder if I can do that.

She conducted more trials. Played. Delighted in her developing ability.

Her cockiness led to the 'I told you so' moment.

She thought herself alone in the hills when she let her senses fly. As she tickled the minds of the creatures around her, she not once sensed the eyes that watched or judged. Never suspected the gaze that assessed.

She never knew someone was there, but that was no excuse. Nor did her ignorance save her. She only wished her folly hadn't cost her father's life. How she would have given anything to hear him say, "I told you so," one more time.

The masked kidnappers came for her in the darkest hour of night, dragging her from her bed despite her shrill cries for aid. "Papa. Papa. Help me."

But her father couldn't save her. He'd not even been able to save himself.

Layla did her best to escape, blasting forth with her untrained power, seeking help, but in the end, an unschooled girl, even with a small herd of spitting cats and cackling hens rampaging, was no match for grown men. In a cruel twist, the avian animals who came to her aid were shot down, plucked and roasted.

Even worse, while they smelled great roasting over an open fire, they tasted even better with salt and a dash of pepper.

With no regard to her wishes, she was taken captive and her new life began. A prisoner treated like a prized goose, she was sold to the highest bidder. More than a slave, not quite a servant, she was both treasure and tool.

Her first owner placed chains around her, real ones made of gold. Much like a songbird, he caged her and then lived to regret it, as did those who served him as. During her first incarceration, she taught more than one person to fear the chirp of a canary. They might seem small and cute, but a flock of them could cause serious damage.

It seemed she didn't take well to having her freedom curtailed, but that didn't stop her capture and sale to the next highest bidder. It didn't take long after her new keeper locked her away before she embarked upon what she now fondly recalled as Escape #2. An escape of opportunity.

Given the lack of actual planning and her by-the-seat-of-her-pants execution, it was almost surprising how far she made it and for how long. While her first bout for freedom lasted less than twenty-four hours, she learned from her mistakes. Escape #2 netted her six months of glorious freedom.

Until, once again, her cockiness got her in trouble. An article in a newspaper led the hunter to her.

A gang of cats, yes cats, are engaging in thievery. Several surveillance cameras have shown the feline burglars absconding with the oddest items. Clothing, food, and, in the weirdest twist yet, a team of them made off with a comforter. Evolution of the cat? Behaviorists don't know.

Unfortunately, her army of felines and their acts didn't go unnoticed. *Oops.*

So much for Escape #2. Off she went to her third owner, who didn't believe in gold cages, but her next room, with its barred windows and door, wasn't much of an improvement. Thus did she hatch, Escape #3, rise of the rats.

Chapter One

I don't know how those cats find this comfortable.

Tree branches did not make the most pleasant of seats, especially if sat on for several hours.

Normally, Brody wouldn't be found perched in a tree like a pea-brained bird. He preferred to keep his two feet—or four paws—on the ground. But he had a good reason for hiding in the treetop. As to how he got there, it had started hours before.

It started with him waking early. Brody never woke early. He was a sleep-in-late, hit-the-snooze-button-a-few-times kind of guy. But at the ungodly hour of nine a.m., he rolled out of bed. He was in the office by ten a.m., which caused his alpha, Reid, to question if he was all right.

No. No, I'm not. Restlessness plagued him, an unease and sense that something was amiss.

At first, he blamed it on too much coffee. For some reason, shifters didn't process caffeine as quickly as other drugs. An odd trait.

Three cups, strong enough to make him sprout hair without even trying, and Jan tossed him out of the office claiming if he didn't stop pacing she was going to shoot him and use his fur to make a jacket. Knowing Jan, she meant every word.

He left and went on the prowl, sniffing every corner in Kodiak Point. *Just doing my job.* As clan Beta, it fell upon him to ensure things ran smoothly and to note potential issues that might affect the safety or well-being of the clan. If something cropped up, he could either take care of the issue or report the problem to Reid. *But not kill it.* He was living in the civilized world now.

Boring. So, so boring, but safe. No one was shooting at him. He ate regularly, got more sleep than needed. Could shower whenever.

Which totally sucked.

A man craved a bit of excitement in his life.

Whatever plagued his gut—which never steered him wrong and always knew when someone was hosting a barbecue—he didn't sniff it out in town. So Brody roamed farther, leaving the civilized areas—a bit of a misnomer really given the wild shifters living in the homes—and took to the woods.

This time of the year, with so much daylight, life abounded, from the green leafy kind to the four-legged and furry. Insects thrived too, much to his irritation. He slapped at yet another mosquito determined to suck him dry. Mini vampire bastards.

Of all his abilities as a Lycan—another name for wolf shifters—the one he would have really appreciated was one to counteract the itchiness of insect bites. He'd be scratching up a storm later, which meant he'd have to put up with

Boris needling him about getting a flea collar.

Stupid moose thought he was so funny. Funny was Brody spraying silly string at Boris' antlers and hearing him bellow. A beautiful moment caught forever on video.

Scratching aside, Brody couldn't complain about the other benefits of being a Lycan, such as quick healing, great health, a resistance to most diseases, and, of course, a kickass timber wolf he could swap into.

Hey, let's not forget my awesome hair. A shaggy mane, which he kept long on his head, possibly in a fuck-you gesture to his old sergeant who thought the only proper hair cut was a bald one.

Bzzz. Another winged leech died. Ten more took its place.

Given the insect problem, Brody could have shed his skin and let his thicker pelt protect him, but he decided to hold off. For one thing, his wolf form emitted a much stronger, noticeable scent, and his second reason was instinct, which said he needed to exercise patience, not something his beast side was known for.

Wait? Why wait? Hate watching. We need to act.

Say hello to his impulsive wolf. His Lycan side did so hate inaction, and yet most of Brody's missions involved patience. Observation and planning. Then, when the right moment arrived, pounce on opportunity—which in most cases meant kick some ass.

Those were times his wolf lived for. Thrived. In the past, most of Brody's assignments involved violence—and that was when his wolf got to come out and play.

But this wasn't wolf time. And this wasn't war. This was Kodiak Point, and for the moment, it was watch and wait time.

No biting?

No biting.

A grown wolf shouldn't use puppy eyes on its human host. Good thing Brody was immune. He stayed two-legged and decided to find himself a hiding spot in the woods. His options?

Tree. Other tree. Bush. Smaller bush. Big tree.

No surprise, he went with the big tree in order to properly mask his presence. He needed something far from the ground, the higher, the better. Since most of the attacks involved shifters, many of whom possessed a keen nose, it was best to take every precaution.

Including one that reeked. Literally.

Time to spritz himself with his lovely cologne, eau de stinky squirrel. Gag.

It was one thing to chase a frisky, furry-tailed creature, another to smell of one. To compound the insult, much like one of those chattering little rodents, he had to climb a tree. Piece of cake—and he knew just the kind. Rum-soaked chocolate cake with whipped cream between the layers and crushed cherries. Drool. Aunt Betty-Sue—who wasn't his aunt but insisted with a wag of her spoon that he call her that—made him one every year for his birthday.

It took him but a moment to clamber his chosen aerie—while wondering if he texted Aunt

Betty-Sue whether she'd bake one for him just for the hell of it. The woman loved to cook, and he loved to eat. It was a great friendship—especially since it gave him opportunities, behind Betty-Sue's back, to taunt her son, Travis, mercilessly. And got the grizzly in trouble when he retaliated. Hehehe.

For his hiding spot, Brody chose an old Sitka Spruce, which towered well over a hundred feet and provided ample cover. The branches were thick and sturdy.

Brody did his best to climb while disrupting as little as possible. Nothing like a shower of greenery at the base of a tree to announce the presence of something overhead.

The branch he chose was fat enough to hide him if he sat still. From his vantage point, he could glimpse parts of the town laid out before him and perhaps catch an early peek at whatever was setting off his danger meter.

Let it be something good.

Edible, added his wolf.

Brody would settle for anything if he got to act.

Hours passed. The sun blazed, and nothing happened except for the irritated squeak of a squirrel acting territorial. Stupid creature dared to chatter at him, so Brody showed it some lip and growled. It wisely scooted away.

It was the most exciting thing to happen so far.

Hunger made his belly rumble. He ignored it. He'd gone longer without food in the past. Besides, Betty-Sue had texted him to say she'd not only made him a cake—fist pump—she'd left him a lasagna in his fridge since she accidentally made an extra.

The knowledge almost had him abandoning his observation post. The cruelty of having to wait.

He fought the temptation. He did, however, sip sparingly from his flask, water, not booze. A wolf never drank on the job. But after? He could totally picture getting rip-roaring drunk and singing off key.

Time rolled by without any action. The evening glared bright, the sun unwilling to lose its grip. Welcome to Alaska in the summer time when daylight reigned supreme. Eventually, as the hour grew late, the mighty sun finally deigned to dive down past the horizon for a respite.

And that was when Brody's hours of silent watching and waiting paid off.

No sooner did the dark of night envelop the land than the figures came slinking, proving his gut right yet again. *I've still got the knack.*

At first, they crept in single digits; a lone wolf here, a jackrabbit there, a man, who was more than a man and who never once bothered to look up.

Idiot.

Anyone so lax wouldn't prove much of a challenge. Good thing a couple of the interloper's buddies accompanied him on his stealthy trek toward town. They definitely emitted a seriously nefarious vibe.

Or, as was known in the Lycan world, promising a violently good time.

What a way to celebrate the solstice. Once he got out of the tree. Preferably alive.

The numbers were kind of against him. It wouldn't do to get noticed while he was here alone. Besides, think of the fun when he snuck up behind them and howled an attack.

Since Brody didn't dare inhale too deeply, or do anything that might emit the slightest sound lest he give his presence away, this meant he couldn't identify what caste the slinking strangers belonged to, but he would have wagered his favorite knife—the blade sharp enough to shave with—that at least one of the males who'd gone by was some kind of ocean shifter. Maybe seal.

Bleh. Want red meat. His wolf had a definite preference. Maybe Brody would save that one for Gene, whose polar bear really enjoyed the occasional blubbery treat, with pepper. As for Brody? The only good seafood came with a shell, roasted over an open fire with a butter sauce for dipping.

The salty-smelling fellow didn't travel alone. While those on two legs were few in number— from what Brody could discern from his perch, for all he knew there were dozens a few hundred leagues over approaching from the north—the wild beasts who accompanied the enemy shifters numbered in the dozens. Probably more given Brody could only spot a small section.

And still no audible warning from any of the sentries.

The town was about to be attacked, and yet, not a single sentry cried out. Not a single flare lit the sky in warning.

Slackers.

A good thing Brody had staked himself in the tree long enough to spy them, else the town would have been caught unprepared. But better than saving the day, he'd get to fight.

I'm gonna get to hit something.

Awoo.

Yes, he was excited. Brody craved the adrenaline of battle, and not just because he enjoyed hitting things. Keeping his skills honed took practice, but testing their efficiency required an opponent.

And lucky him, he already had more than enough sneaking in from the northern section of these woods, an area that shouldn't have any kind of foot traffic.

How did they make it past the sentries? And, damn, will Gene be pissed about this.

The head of defensive perimeter, Gene had spent the last few weeks revamping their early-warning system. They'd needed it.

Some prick kept attempting to weaken the clan, to cause trouble. Sneaky shifters kept stealing while weirdly trained wildlife kept attacking in small spurts. Sure, a snarling raccoon on his own wasn't a big deal, but a swarm of them? The women of town would have warm hands this winter with all the new mittens they'd be making.

So far, the people—snicker, okay, maybe he should call them what they were, shifters—of Kodiak Point smacked down the assault by the oddly trained wild creatures each time. However, so far, most of the incursions were small and easily rebuffed. In the case of the rarer large attacking groups, they'd received advance warning of incoming trouble from the sentries.

Sentries that were currently silent despite the several two—and four—legged bodies he could see.

If the boys on duty weren't already dead, they'd wish they were once Brody got through with them. Those guarding the borders to their clan land were supposed to raise the alarm at the slightest hint of anything hinky. Judging by the shadows that crept in under the cover of darkness, they'd failed.

Or they were dead.

In which case, I will avenge you.

Given the number of enemy he'd seen pass by, this was the battle they'd waited for.

On the eve of the summer solstice, only a few scant hours of night existed, a short window to launch a furtive attack. The ambushers knew enough of their defenses to either avoid or take out their early-warning system. Someone planned well.

But not well enough.

The clan would meet the ambush because Brody would make sure of it. Muting the glow of his screen by tucking it inside his jacket, he fired off a quick text to Reid, Gene, and Boris.

ATK—short for "We're under attack, get everyone's ass ready and armed."

Awoo. Party in the village tonight. *Sorry, you sneaky suckers, but you're about to get a nasty surprise.*

Fun fun fun! But only if he ever got out of

the bloody tree.

When the last of the sneaky varmints passed under his unnoticed watch point, Brody swung himself down, dropping as silently as possible. The last thing he needed was for those who'd recently passed to hear him and turn around.

Some might have questioned his courage at not confronting the hoard, and to them, he said piss off. Only a stupid man attacked when the numbers were against him. Actually, not entirely true. Gene never calculated the odds. When that big-ass bear went into a berserker rage, he had no concept of odds. It was probably one of his more endearing traits.

Smarts kept Brody from attacking, but never fear. When the time came, he would join the battle and rank high when it came to his share of kills. After all, he did have a reputation as a bad-ass wolf to maintain and a certain moose to put in his place. *All about the rack indeed.*

It was time to put those who thought their antlers were so mighty in their place. Never doubt the power of fur and fang.

With his feet on the ground, and the attackers well out of sight, Brody wasted no time, shedding his clothes and tossing them at the base of the tree before letting his flesh ripple and his shape twist until he stood in his four-legged form. He stretched, a mighty timber wolf with brindled fur, sharp teeth, and a howl that could carry for miles.

Antlers can't do that. But they did make great chandeliers. Odd how Boris didn't appreciate the ornate one Brody had sent him on his birthday. Ungrateful moose.

Sucking in a deep breath, Brody howled, an ululating cry meant to warn any inhabitants still slumbering or unaware.

Someone heard his warning and passed the message along. The quiet of night soon filled with snarls and roars as his kin, not military trained and less prone to quiet, prepared to meet the menace threatening them.

Welcome to Kodiak Point. We might seem civilized from the outside, but threaten us and we will tear your throat out. And that was just the men.

The women could prove even more vicious if you threatened their cubs and pups. Brody didn't know a woman in town who didn't have some kind of recipe passed down to deal with naughty kin. Brody's grandfather used to lament the good old days when one of the most sought after delicacies was Traitor Tourtière—an old recipe from some French settlers that relied on several species donating some meat. Lest you think his grandfather was an utter carnivore, keep in mind the pie also sported a thick, flaky crust and potatoes—soaked in the juices of lots of meat. Tongue lolling.

Satisfied the town was alert and ready to meet the charge of attackers, Brody prepared to rush the enemy from behind, only to stop as an unusual scent caught his attention.

Exotic.   Sweet.   And   mysteriously compelling.

What is that smell?

It blew to him from the north on the wings of a gentle breeze. The brush of it across his nose teased and distracted him. He didn't recognize it, but he knew enough to wager it wasn't human, not entirely. Nor was it animal. So what did that leave?

Did it matter?

The enemy was closing in on the town he called home. Did he really have time to chase down strange smells?

Could he afford to ignore it?

Hadn't his sarge said, "Never let something inexplicable go uninspected," especially when it came to reconnoitering?

So long as sniffing away from the main trail didn't affect a current, time-sensitive mission, then the hunting down of the unusual was encouraged. After all, sometimes it took only one clue to stop a war.

And the clan was on the verge of war.

Screw verge, they were about to engage in one given the numbers now approaching the outskirts of town.

But who was the one behind it?

In the last year, while the clan of Kodiak Point had repelled more than their fair share of attacks and problems, they'd yet to catch a glimpse of the perpetrator.

No one knew who he was.

No one remembered his face.

And no one had a name.

What if the odor belonged to the mastermind behind the violent acts being perpetrated against them? What if this scent, this oddity in the forest, was a clue and the chance they'd waited for to take out, once and for all, the mysterious figure fucking with their lives?

Tough decision.

Fight or explore?

He knew his wolf's answer. And it wasn't easy keeping those four feet planted while he took an extra moment to analyze his choices.

Argh. Both were so tempting. Maybe he didn't have to choose. First part of the mission, capture the weird smell, then, in phase two, hopefully catch the tail end of the fight.

I'll have my lasagna, my cake, and knowing aunt Betty-Sue once the violence is over with, the stove will go on, and we'll all have pie, too.

Since Brody didn't want to leave all his gear behind, especially in case he needed his phone or the cuffs, he shifted back to his man shape. He pulled his pants back on but left off the shirt and shoes. He'd move more silently on bare feet. The gun he tucked in the waistband of his jeans, and his knapsack—which he'd stuffed with cuffs, water, and his phone and also held some rope good for hog tying and hangings—was slung on one shoulder.

He fired off another text to Reid; *Wrd sml. Ck.* Translation: *I smell something weird and am checking it out.*

Reid's superb reply. *K. Bt u. Okay, but you do know this means I'll totally ream you in battle kills.*

Argh. He would, but that was okay. Brody could totally still win the day if he caught someone of import. Head honcho was worth a hundred minion points if counting.

The teasing scent grew stronger as Brody padded through the trees, ghosting much like Gene amongst the foliage. Leaving no trace of his passage and downwind, thus not announcing his presence, Brody stalked his prey.

The tantalizing aroma increased in potency, and still he couldn't decipher it.

Did it have a hint of cinnamon? He inhaled. Yes, but also a bit of a flowery taint, jasmine if he remembered his botany classes correctly. Which wasn't some stale course taken within the tame confines of a greenhouse. Oh no. Brody learned his greenery out in the field, sometimes blindfolded by his sarge, who would bark at Brody and the other soldiers that they were poisoned and needed to find a particular plant as antidote.

Such great memories, like the time Sarge saved Brody's life after he realized Brody had chosen the wrong plant and ingested actual poison. The rhino didn't hesitate to act. He also didn't waste the opportunity to teach the other soldiers a lesson. Using Brody's body as a dummy, he detailed how to purge a victim.

Ah, the good old days.

The scent wafting on the breeze wasn't a toxin. He would have wagered his life on it. Cinnamon and jasmine. Mixed together it proved an exotic perfume. A palate-tempting one.

It also compelled him.

Drew him.

Practically drugged him.

What. The. Fuck.

He shook his head to clear it as he realized he'd stumbled along, without a care, la-de-da, stepping like a drunken, clod-footed moose toward the source.

This wasn't like him. Brody stopped his feet, even though they insisted on moving. His whole body leaned toward the direction of the scent.

How unnatural and freaky.

Not a poison, but the scent is certainly some form of attractant. Which never boded well.

Only the most deadly of plants or creatures ever emitted that type of odorous trap. Whatever oozed it now did not belong in these woods, which meant, more than ever, Brody needed to track the source, but at the same time, he needed to figure out how to prevent the smell from affecting him.

He needed a counteragent.

Pretty smell meet bad one.

Brody pulled his squirrel cologne out, a small atomizer atop a glass vial. So innocuous in appearance, and yet the murky yellow liquid held within was capable of transforming his manly wolf scent—which the ladies loved—into something else. The rank stench liberally dabbed under his nose destroyed his current ability to smell.

Eew. Nasty. Not exactly pleasant, but it helped dispel the lingering effect that drew him like a drone toward the smell that didn't belong in these woods. *What, or who, is it?*

As he continued on his way, creeping silently now instead of mindlessly, Brody noticed some oddities around him. For one, he wasn't the only one drawn in that direction. Rodents of all castes scampered ahead of him.

His wolf watched them avidly through his eyes. He also flashed a visual commentary that went along the lines of, *Snack. Snack. Almost a lunch.*

His wolf practically slobbered at the buffet. Brody preferred his meat from the store. It was less work to prepare.

While he couldn't see them, Brody heard the flutter of wings as avian creatures swept overhead. Hopefully not bats. He disliked bats, and he had ever since he encountered that flock of blood-sucking ones when on a mission in the rain forest. *Don't attack humans, my ass.* They sure as hell had no problem with shifters.

Hate them. And they taste bad too.

The fact that even roasted over a campfire, basted with lemon juice, didn't make them palatable didn't answer the question of the moment.

What the hell is going on?

Reid would want to know. Hell, Brody wanted to know.

The only time animals ran in a herd with a single purpose was if danger swept from behind them. Usually fire, although, occasionally, a giant Yeti would venture from the ice fields and give the local inhabitants a good scare.

Fun times for Brody and the others though.

The farther he went, the more the trees tapered, leaving him with scarce cover. But it didn't stop him from following the trail of little creatures as they flowed past him to congregate in a cleared area from which thrust a rocky outcropping.

As clearings went, this one wasn't special. It didn't have any Stonehenge type monoliths or ancient burial ground. The rocky mound was comprised of boulders of varying size, which had no cultural significance. Until now.

Now it was a throne, an island amidst an undulating sea of furry, writhing bodies, all jostling for a spot before the rocks.

But why?

Lest he crush tiny bodies, Brody halted and took stock. With the moon at its smallest wedge, there wasn't much illumination, but his wolf side made up for it and allowed him to make out some of the details, enough to note that amongst the mice and squirrels and other small forest denizens were larger ones such as a coon and a fox—not the intelligent or related-to-Jan kind.

But the animals weren't the most interesting thing.

She was.

Atop the boulders sat a woman, a seemingly human one. A woman seated on a rocky throne, whose presence drew him.

A shiver went through him like he'd not experienced in all his years, not even in the military. Something about the way she sat, the way the animals all seemed to gather in reverence, really bothered him. It totally set off his whig-o-meter.

What. The. Fuck.

Now this is what his sarge would have classified as interesting.

He moved closer, not even trying to hide,

wanting a better glimpse of her before he acted. She seemed utterly oblivious to his presence.

Like hello. Big bad wolf here.

Big bad wolf who smelled like an itty bitty squirrel.

Okay, so he'd give her a pass on smelling his presence. But still. What about her other senses? Did she not sense danger gazing upon her?

I am here. Hear me howl. Awoo!

Not a twitch.

Oblivious about his arrival or choosing to ignore him? He'd wager a bit of both.

Weird, but not as weird as the fact all the forest animals seemed to gaze upon her with utter adoration.

Talk about really fucking freaky.

Now, if he were Boris or Gene, he'd have probably hauled out his gun and shot her. His old army buddies lived by very simple rules: *If you don't like it, kill it.*

But, unlike Kyle and his crown of antlers, Brody tried to use his head for more than just a hat rack. It saw the woman, sitting crossed-legged atop the outcropping, her head tilted back, hair fluttering in a whirling breeze, forming a nimbus around her crown, and he thought, *Interesting.*

As part of education in the spy arts, his sarge taught him to not kill interesting things unless he really had to. *Keep the person of interest alive,* he'd drilled. Bring them back for questioning. Ask them if they had something to do with the feral creatures of late who'd banded together and attacked the residents of Kodiak Point.

Mission objective—capture the woman for questioning.

First phase: how to get to her? And without drawing undue attention.

For the moment, his target seemed oblivious to his presence, but that could quickly change. Brody wished he'd thought to bring a tranquilizer gun with him. Alas, he had only his knife and a regular pistol. *And some cuffs.* If he could get close enough, given his size advantage, he could surely subdue her and slip them on.

But that required him approaching, which meant he'd have to either find a way around the furry sea, or he'd have to crush them. Not usually a squeamish guy, even Brody had to balk at the idea of stomping the little creatures. Yet what choice did he truly have?

Sidling to the left while keeping her in sight, he barely dared to blink, lest she disappear again. He sought a clear path or at least one less rife with bodies. None appeared. She was like an isle amongst the creatures come to pay whisker-twitching homage.

When no easy route availed itself, he realized there was nothing he could do. Wrinkling his nose in disgust, he stepped forward.

No crunch. He dared a peek down. The writhing bodies had parted for his foot. He watched as he lifted the other and aimed it over a few heads. They didn't run. They didn't squeak. How utterly uncanny. Yet, as his foot descended, they flowed out of the way, giving him a clear spot to land his toes.

I am that bearded fellow from that Bible except I'm parting the furry sea.

Brody made his way to the rocks without doing any damage. As soon as he proved close enough, he leapt on to a boulder, his bare toes gripping the rough surface. He glanced at his target to check on her status.

During his entire trek, she hadn't moved. Her head still remained thrust back, and her hair danced wildly, snapping as if alive with static electricity. For all he knew she was electric. The air this close to her definitely hummed, almost creating a music, one that vibrated against the edges of his consciousness.

He ignored it as he crept closer. The creepy situation didn't improve when he noted her eyes were wide open but rolled back, displaying only the white orbs. Totally not cool.

While not a big watcher of horror movies, even Brody knew there was something supernatural about the whole situation. He could hear Boris grunting, "Kill it."

But he couldn't. Murder a seemingly unarmed woman, alone on a rocky perch?

It was too easy.

Way too easy.

And not right.

Who and what is she?

He both wanted to know and, at the same time, desperately wanted to run away.

Ever had the feeling your life was about to drastically change? Yeah, he had that feeling, and he didn't like it one bit. Problem was uneasiness didn't mean he'd take the coward's route.

Brody lived for danger. Reveled in it. And this situation screamed danger, despite its benign appearance thus far.

Despite the teeth-thrumming vibe coming off the woman, he crept as close as he could to her prone figure. He took a deep breath and then wrapped his arms around her. A jolt of awareness slammed into him. It stole most of his breath, leaving him only with enough to mutter, "Gotcha."

Yet he couldn't help but think he was the one captured instead.

Chapter Two

The moment he made his decision to approach she was aware of him. All of the animals in the clearing were.

Predator. He's come among us. Run. Hide. Eek!

The simple minds quavered in fear, and yet she held them tight. It drained her awfully to expend so much of her will and over such a vast area, but at the same time, how free she felt.

So many sensations bombarded her, not hers, the animals. With but a touch of her mind, and a yank at their will, she could live through their eyes. Feel through their paws. Die during a futile attack.

She'd already withdrawn her consciousness out of the creatures attacking Kodiak Point. She'd gotten them there, given them the order to attack, but she wouldn't watch through their eyes or suffer as they got injured or died. She'd seen too much death already.

Besides, the real reason for her presence approached. *He's behind me. He's—*

Even though Layla had expected his touch, she couldn't help a gasp when he grabbed her. She certainly never expected the flash of heat his contact would bring—nor how pleasant she would find it.

Awareness flared to life, not the adrenaline-filled kind brought upon by the threat of danger, but the more erotic type. The awareness of a woman for a man, not something she'd truly experienced much, but given how much romance she read, definitely recognizable. Her captor exuded a certain aura—confidence, strength, masculinity—and it shocked her when she responded to it, responded to him, a stranger.

"Gotcha!" The man's warm breath fluttered by the lobe of her ear. It started a chain reaction, shooting a shiver straight through the length of her. *If only you did have me.*

Because he was mistaken in who was truly captured. While the wolf might hold her, he would never get the chance to keep her.

The master had plans for the shapeshifter, plans she could state with a degree of certainty wouldn't end well for the guy.

Another waste of a life to satisfy the sadistic nature of the master—the title was his idea. Someone had delusions of grandeur and wasn't afraid to kill to achieve it.

"You should run now while you can." She tried to warn him. Her stab at rebellion.

As expected, he didn't listen. "Not likely, sweetheart." He hugged her tighter, and silly her, she enjoyed it.

I am such a slut for attention. How desperate am I that I feel such excitement for a stranger?

Smarten up. She wasn't here to enjoy

herself. She was but a tool in an arsenal for revenge, and, if she completed this task, she'd be rewarded with a mixed bag of junk food. To those who took freedom for granted and judged her for being bought so cheaply, try pacing the interior of her ten-by-ten cage for a year before judging her.

She'd do almost anything for a few pounds of chocolate or an excursion outside where she could breathe fresh air or feel sunlight on her skin.

In this case, to receive her reward, all she had to do was send some simple wolves and other creatures—not many given they'd already cleared most of the area in previous attacks—to assist an ambush on the town. Easy. Just like it was easy to set herself up as bait on the rock.

Sit and play with the animals. Those were the orders. Let her innate power draw all to her, including a curious wolf.

Her master had a specific goal in mind when he outlined the plan, such an intricate plot just to get to this point. The attack on the town, a feeble ploy to draw attention away from the true purpose today. Capture a wolf.

The targeted shifter walked, unsuspecting, into the trap, a trap about to snap shut. She could almost feel sorry for him, but his life versus hers and a pillowcase of chocolate?

Was it selfish? That depended. Was it selfish to want to protect herself?

Still, though, it didn't make the guilt any less. She turned her vivid purple gaze his way, their startling color in her tanned complexion always throwing newcomers for a loop.

Her tone wasn't the least bit triumphant when she said, "I'm sorry, sir wolf, but it is not I who is captive, but you."

While her brand of animal magic wouldn't work on him—his mind was too strong for that—the dart that struck from the shadows was made to take out even the toughest predator. The second, third, and fourth tufted dart were precautions.

His eyes widened as he slurred, "Bloody hell." That was all he managed to utter before the strong sleeping agent put him out.

The arms around her slackened, but before the guy could topple them from their precarious perch, figures appeared, their dark clothing making them seem like shadows come to life.

The master's men plucked the guy's limp body from the rock and slapped silver cuffs on him, the metal painful to the touch and impossible for him to break.

Almost she could feel sorry for the man. He'd not asked to get caught. He'd done nothing to deserve his capture. Yet, when he next awoke, the freedom he'd enjoyed would be denied.

Welcome to my world.

A world where all obeyed the dictates of the master or face the consequences. But at least he served good food. A well-fed slave was a strong one, capable of wreaking havoc in his master's name. Or so she'd heard like a zillion times.

Villains tended to stick to well-known speeches she'd noticed.

Speak of the devil… "Well done, my pet." His robotic words grated on the ear.

"As if I had a choice," she muttered to the robed figure, who didn't so much as walk in to the clearing as flow.

The animals she'd used to help draw the wolf had scattered as soon as she stopped humming. The spell that bound them quickly dissipated, and given their status as prey, their protective instincts quickly kicked in. All that remained to remind of their presence was trampled greenery and one comatose guy who would awake to doom.

How ominous. A dire soundtrack of duhn-duhn-duhn played in her head.

"Sassy words will get you punished, pet."

Blah. Blah. "Name something that doesn't," she replied, not cowed in the least.

The master had tried to get her to show respect. Over and over. He'd quickly discovered that, while he could punish her body, her spirit refused to be quelled.

Layla wouldn't allow it. She held tight to the hope and belief that one day she would escape— *I'm sure Escape #57 is the one.* Yes, she'd kept count over the last few years. She'd learned from each one of her failures.

Don't hitchhike wearing only a thin gown.

Don't forget to get the key first before killing your jailor.

Don't eat the pretty red berries on the bush in the woods unless you need to lose weight.

"You're ignoring me," he snapped.

Such an attention whore. "I did what you asked. Give me my chocolate."

"And if I don't?"

"Then you'd better kill me because you remember what happened the last time you reneged on a deal." She went on a hunger strike and refused to do anything.

He'd had to postpone his plans, which didn't please him at all.

"I should beat you for your impertinence." Should, but wouldn't. Oh, he would hurt her, make no mistake, but he wouldn't kill her or do anything to severely harm her for fear of losing her ability.

So long as she proved useful, he held back.

But she wasn't holding back. Not anymore.

Of late, she'd been pushing at that invisible line that kept the master from snapping. Pushed and pushed, tired of waiting for rescue to come. Tired of a life spent living in a cage.

Escape #57. It was the lucky number. The one that would finally succeed. She just knew it.

If not, she heard fifty-eight made a good digit.

Chapter Three

Waking groggy and on the floor? Hadn't happened in years.

Must have been some good shit.

Wait a second, he'd neither smoked nor drank anything. This wasn't a hangover.

I was fucking drugged.

How embarrassing. Like a green-nosed recruit, Brody had sauntered into a trap. He'd never live it down. Boris would make sure of it.

Of course, in order to hear the mockery, first Brody had to escape. Placing himself in a seated position, Brody took stock of his situation.

Cliché was the word that came to mind as he glanced around. Standard cement block basement with an old coal furnace in a corner, its belly currently cold this time of year. Scattered around were stacks of boxes, the mildewed cardboard bulging as dampness and neglect took its toll.

On a wall across from him sat a vintage puke-green washer from the seventies with a knob missing on its display panel, but he'd wager the beast still worked. Those old machines were built to last. A more recent-model white dryer shared a spot alongside, its front panel spotted with rust. To finish off the wondrously uninviting space? A giant cage with him smack-dab in the middle of it.

Because no basement was complete without a prison cell.

For the moment, Brody appeared alone and in surprisingly good shape. Nothing broken, no puddles of blood, no screaming pain in any parts of his body. However, he wasn't entirely untouched.

What's this around my neck? Cold and heavy, it seemed someone had given him some jewelry. His fingers explored the metal band ringing his neck.

Argh. Someone collared me.

Was it childish to want to make choking noises? Probably, and he did restrain himself, but his wolf felt no such need and whined pitifully in his mind.

A wolf could handle plenty of things. However, he'd never willingly give up his freedom.

Getting caught was embarrassing, and Brody could see he'd have to work on escape if he intended to maintain his man card in good standing.

Time to give this contraption the slip.

He felt along the tubular metal ring, searching for a clasp. Only smooth metal met his touch. Seamlessly joined with no hint of a button or trigger.

It's getting tighter, whined his wolf.

It wasn't, but the setback of not quickly removing it didn't sit well. Brody needed to try something different. Given he was stronger than the average man, he'd snap the fucking thing. Slipping his fingers around the ring, he tugged. He twisted. He cursed a storm—in more than one language.

The damned necklace wouldn't come off.

Ack. Gurgle. His wolf collapsed into a mentally traumatized heap.

Brody almost laughed.

You are such a drama king.

His wolf gave him the mental equivalent of the evil eye.

This did make Brody chuckle.

Most shifters were close to their animals, but not all of them considered it a best friend and held actual conversations with it. Okay, more like visualizations since his wolf couldn't speak words. But via flashes of images and actions, his beast could get his point across.

This understanding didn't come easily.

Brody really began to connect with his wolf during his longest incarceration. The solitude made for ideal meditation conditions and total mental openness. Open enough to meet his other side and truly come to an understanding.

Brody often credited this unique bond as the reason he'd emerged less damaged than his brothers after his solitary confinement at the hands of the rebels. Don't get him wrong, he still remembered it with utmost clarity, but given how long ago it had happened, Brody tried to not reflect on it. He'd moved on, even if some of his brothers hadn't.

Reminiscing about the past wouldn't help

the current situation, nor would placating his wolf over their newest accessory.

"Sorry, buddy," Brody said aloud. "But the jewelry stays for now. We've got other shit to worry about." Such as himself. Was the collar the only thing he now sported? Any more surprises?

A quick grab of his manparts showed them intact.

Big sigh of relief.

Apparel-wise, Brody still wore his jeans, albeit with empty pockets. No surprise, the gun he kept tucked in the back was gone, as was the knife he'd strapped to his ankle. He remained shirtless, his upper body bare to the cool air of the dank space. It didn't bother him. He lived in Alaska for fuck's sake. It got a lot colder than this in the winter, even with clothes.

Twisting to review what he could of his back, and craning to check his torso, he didn't see anything of concern. Other than a few light bruises and contusions from his manhandling, he appeared no worse for wear.

Clue: whoever captured him wanted him alive for some purpose. That worked for him. An undamaged and conscience wolf was a plotting one. *I've yet to meet a prison that can hold me.*

And he'd done time in his fair share while conducting his various missions. Lock picking was one of his many skills. Give him something pin-like and he'd have those lock tumblers dancing in no time.

Except this cage didn't bear a lock. Approaching the bars where he could see the reinforced outline of a door, he tried to spot the locking mechanism. It only concerned him a little when he couldn't see one. That might prove a challenge, even with his talents.

He'd still prevail. All prisons had a flaw. He just had to find it. He'd done it before in the prison overseas, the one he occupied the longest. In the end, it couldn't hold him.

Before Brody could reach through the bars and palpate the area around where he'd usually find a lock, he heard the squeak of a door opening. A shaft of daylight illuminated the upper part of a wooden staircase tucked in an opposite corner. When he didn't note anything to use as a weapon, he crouched, hands tucked at his side, his entire body ready to spring into action—or to morph into almost two hundred pounds of furry menace.

He noted toes first then an ankle. Brody glimpsed most of a calf, too, before the edge of a gown hid the rest. A shame. Bared thighs were a favorite of his. Some guys like breasts or ass, but Brody, he liked a rounded pair of thighs, thighs he could grip.

Except in this case, the only grip he should contemplate was a hand around her neck.

Her.

Down the stairs, head bowed as if watching her steps, descended the woman from the rock. *If it isn't my friend, Bait.* Bait that he'd fallen for.

He snarled. "You." He didn't hide his irritation. Let her realize she'd messed with the wrong dude.

Uncoiling himself, he rose to his full height

and approached the bars, grabbing them just as she cried out, "Don't."

Sizzle. Burning smell. No frying pan or bacon in sight.

Hmmm. Probably not a good sign.

He yanked his burning hands away from the silver-coated bars. Too late. They were throbbing an angry red. Fuck. That would hurt as it healed.

With the introduction of the silver, the level of difficulty when it came to escape went up. But he'd still prevail. Especially if he could get his hands on the woman who'd dangled herself like a juicy steak.

He glared at her. She didn't seem intimidated in the least, probably because she had a couple of burly guards at her back. One was skinny as hell, tall though, with long, lanky hair that straggled over his face. The other fellow was shorter but wide and, with his wide forehead, Neanderthal looking. Stickboy and Caveman.

We could totally take them and feast for lunch.

And have the girl for dessert.

Problem was, while he could picture taking down the enforcers, his idea of dessert was less capture of the enemy and more seduction.

Don't fall for her innocent look, soldier. Words he needed to heed.

Gotta get my head in the game.

"Have you come to taunt me?" he growled.

"Hardly," she muttered as she continued to approach him, her bare feet making only the tiniest slapping sound on the dirty concrete floor.

Something about the scenario kept him

from retorting. What was going on here? Why did she seem more prisoner than capturer?

A third pair of booted feet came clattering down the stairs. *Oh look, Jackass is coming to help.* The newest arrival looked kind of donkeyish with his giant front teeth and lumpy body. According to Brody's nose, the guy was human. How interesting. Because Stickboy and Caveman weren't. And neither was the fourth fellow thumping down the stairs.

"Move to the back of the cage," he ordered. Buffalo Jim, a big, barrel-chested dude, sporting a scruffy beard, let his unibrow shrink in a menacing fashion. He also growled for effect.

Oh wait, I think that was supposed to scare me.

Snort.

A human and a dumb bovine plus the two wolves who'd brought the girl down. Four in total and they had their weapons holstered. Even better.

Good odds. He could totally take them.

And then we take the girl.

His wolf heartily approved—just not in the way Brody meant.

You're a dirty dog, Brody chided his inner friend. *I most certainly did not mean we'd take the girl with her skirt around her waist as she claws at my back, panting.* Even if it sounded fun. *She is the enemy.* There was only one place to go once he escaped, back to Kodiak Point, with the girl as his prisoner.

Because good soldiers didn't sleep with the enemy for pleasure.

Although, if she wanted to waste her time trying to use her feminine wiles against him, go ahead. Let her try her damnedest with promises of sex, blowjobs, or even fresh-baked cookies. It wouldn't matter. Brody never compromised his mission, and he wouldn't start now, not even for an attractive woman.

Apparently ignoring Buffalo Jim set off a short—probably caused by penile inadequacy—fuse.

"You were told to move, dog. Now get your ass away from the fucking door before I make you regret it." Said with an impressive wiggle and waggle of the unibrow.

It just made Brody itch for a razor.

Forget his fascination with the furry caterpillar on Buffalo's Jim face. The belligerent idiot had issued him an ultimatum. He knew how to deal with that. Brody's parents taught him to not listen to strangers, and his sarge, that horned bastard, taught him to tell them where to go. "Fuck you. I am not budging."

Of course, a challenge like that worked best if you held the upper hand.

Turned out, he didn't, and they made a liar of him. Brody moved, just not voluntarily.

Thud.

The brand-new necklace he sported served a purpose other than giving him a pimp appearance. It zapped. And he wasn't talking no tiny electrical charge.

Through its conductive surface, it fried him with a steady stream of electricity, enough to send him to his knees, enough to keep him there while the door to the cage opened and the woman was thrust in.

The electrifying experience, which was much on par with getting Tasered, something he'd only experienced once—a training exercise led by his favorite rhino—lasted only until the door slammed shut and was locked again.

Dammit. He missed the tiny details of how it worked, being somewhat distracted by the ongoing jiggle-like-water-on-hot-pavement effect of his electrocution.

Did they use a key? A touch pad? He still didn't know, but he did hear the sound of bolts sliding home.

The current cut off abruptly, but the memory of the pain lingered, leaving him panting on his knees.

Undignified, and unacceptable.

Now that he knew to expect it, he'd react better the next time. Yes, he could almost guarantee a next time. Lots of time spent in various jails didn't mean he'd learned to become a model prisoner. He got punished a lot.

But, for once, it seemed he might get rewarded because the situation had just become extremely interesting. He was still caged, wearing a collar, but he was no longer alone. He shared his cell with a woman. And not just any woman, the woman who'd lured him in to a trap.

"Hello, Bait."

She pursed her lips but didn't reply.

Through the hair that flopped over his eyes, he perused her.

Exotic in appearance, with deeply tanned

skin and raven-dark hair, she was softly curved all over from her plump cheeks and even fuller lips, to the roundness of her bosom lightly hinted at by her linen gown. He couldn't truly discern her body shape, but he'd wager it was hourglass with an indented waist and wide hips. A luscious build, one that would fill a man's hands more than adequately.

Nice mouthful, agreed his wolf.

A gorgeous woman. An enticing one.

One with less-than-human eyes?

What the hell.

No human ever bore the vivid purple of her gaze. The freakish orbs also did not belong to any shapeshifter castes that Brody knew of. And he knew plenty.

Shifters eyes tended to be a variety of colors from a common brown to blue to vivid green and even golden. If stimulated enough, sometimes a hint of otherness would seep through and their gaze would glow to the point they could shine in the darkness.

It totally freaked the enemy out when you did that. More than one soldier had pissed himself when a group of glowing eyes came from the shadows snarling a promise of death.

Ah, the good old days. How he missed them.

Brody was one of the crazy soldiers who'd come home from the war and longed to return. It wasn't that he'd not experienced his share of bad shit during his enlisted service, but more that he thrived on the danger of it. He enjoyed the close comradery he and his soldier brothers shared. The thrill of the chase, of adventure, infused his blood. He was a hunter. A tracker. A wolf.

He was born to seek—and destroy.

Awoo!

Before you got the wrong impression and labeled him a killer, keep in mind, Brody didn't take other lives heedlessly. He did follow a certain code.

Assassination of the enemy for the greater good, totally acceptable.

Kill for fun or pleasure? No, but if you attacked him or those he'd sworn to protect? His feral and wild side would revel in the mayhem.

Forget anything so cliché as calling him the big bad wolf. He was more than that. Brody prided himself as being the ultimate soldier. Spy. Assassin.

Or at least I used to be.

Say hello to the current Kodiak Point clan beta. Boring! Ultimate soldier or not, Brody had retired to remain with his friends who'd emerged from their ordeal a lot more damaged than him. They needed him. So, he got his walking papers from the military and moved to Kodiak Point, small-town boring until recently.

How wrong was it of him to find the recent feints against Reid and the jabs at the inhabitants exciting? *Finally, something to do.*

More interesting than dragging a drunken Eli—who'd shifted into a drunken bald eagle—home, only to have him vomit half digested bug guts and moonshine all over him.

Since the attacks on Kodiak Point began, Brody felt more alive and eager to face the day.

Booyah!

But he was totally getting distracted. Back to his current situation involving a cage and a woman with an unnatural gaze. Those glowing freaking purple eyes totally mesmerized him. Only an idiot would ever mistake this woman for human.

She was also not as innocent as she tried to appear. *Don't forget, she dangled herself like a worm on a hook to capture me.*

He hardened himself against her feminine wiles and decided to attack—verbally. "What the fuck are you?" Not his most elegant of introductions, but then again, whether Bait was beautiful or not, he was kind of pissed at her. *She fooled me.* Never mind his own inattention led to his ignoble capture—which Boris would mock him mercilessly for—she had him drugged, like a common animal!

I am not a simple dog to be put to sleep. Nor was he a greenhorn new to the mercenary game or soldier's battle.

So why had he walked blindly into the trap? He could think of only one reason.

He'd gotten soft during his tenure as beta at Kodiak Point. *I lost my edge.* It was enough to make him want to howl.

Sad awoo. Such a mournful revelation.

Once he escaped—because in his optimistic world, it wasn't a matter of *if* but *when*—he'd have to do something to rectify his complacent attitude. Hone his skills. But for now, he needed to deal with the woman before him, a woman they'd foolishly placed within reach.

A desirable, yummy-smelling, cushy-soft female who, when grabbed and tucked against his body, her round buttocks pressed into his groin, one of his arms around her torso, the other around her neck, caused a total boner moment.

What the fuck!

We do not get aroused during missions.

At least he never had, until now.

Brody had heard of other guys getting hard-ons during skirmishes, but this was a first for him. Given his intense dislike of the woman he held, it disturbed him how attractive she still seemed to his senses. Even his wolf approved. He thought Brody should yank up that skirt on her gown, bend her over and—

Bad wolf.

Chastising his inner wolf for lusting after bait? What was going on? He needed to clear his senses and figure some stuff out, starting with what the hell was this woman? How did she manage to make him react this way?

"I said, what the fuck are you?" He waited for her to answer his question.

She remained silent.

He brought his lips close to her ear and felt her shiver when he whispered. "Silence won't save you. I could kill you in an instant. Snap your neck like a chicken." In reality, he wouldn't. However, she couldn't know that. For so long as she proved possibly useful, she'd get to live. But if she did anything to harm him…

She broke her silence. "I can't answer you,

sir wolf, for I do not know what I am. No one truly does."

"Are you human?" She certainly felt human, her body solid if soft, her plump frame not muscle-bound like most of the women of his acquaintance. She sounded human, her voice a sultry, harmonious tone with a hint of an exotic accent.

Did she derive from some unusual caste overseas that would perhaps explain the cinnamon hint on her skin, the aroma of jasmine delicately woven around it, making her smell entirely too tasty?

We should totally take a lick.

Such a bad wolf.

There would be no licking. Or lusting. And, no, definitely no thrusting. Despite her appearance in his cage, she was the enemy. One did not fornicate with them.

Well…unless it proved truly necessary. A life or death situation came to mind. Then, sleeping with her would be heroic. The things he did to survive war. Sigh. How he missed his old life.

"My father is human."

"But your mother?" he prodded, his lips almost brushing the lobe of her ear. So easy to take a nip.

As if she read his thoughts, her breathing hitched, and the beat of her heart sped up, a rapid flutter almost like that of a trapped animal. It excited his beast.

She licked her lips. "I never knew my mother. She died giving birth to me."

So far, his bullshit detector seemed to think

she spoke the truth. How long would it last? "That's convenient."

"Not really. You try living and not knowing what you are."

"Surely someone in your family knows."

She shook her head.

"What about your father, human or not, he must have had a clue? What about her family? Friends? Someone must have told you something."

The entire time he asked, her head shook. "No. Nothing. It wasn't for lack of trying. My father would only say I was special, just like my mother." She shrugged, the simple motion causing her breasts to momentarily lift then settle against the arm banding her, a simple act he couldn't help but notice.

Definitely more than a handful.

"Get your head in the game!" He could practically hear his old rhino sergeant bark the order. Damn, did he miss the horned bastard. He really should go back for a visit.

"I take it you're not denying there's something different about you?"

"I'd say that was pretty obvious." Such sarcasm from a woman who should have trembled in fear.

Yet, she did tremble a bit. Just not out of trepidation. Did she fight the same bodily awareness he did?

She's the enemy. Remember that. Mutually attracted or not, he mustn't lose sight of what she was.

"What is it you do? I saw those animals in

that clearing. Something was wrong with them. And you…" He recalled the odd vibrating hum that originated from her. "You had something to do with it."

"I did."

What, she didn't even make him work for the reply? He'd totally expected her to deny it.

What was her game? *Because she's certainly thrown mine.* "Mind explaining a bit more."

"Ever heard of the Pied Piper?"

"It's like a nursery rhyme or story or something."

"It's a legend that dates back a few centuries."

"I thought he was a guy, and you—" He paused as he squeezed her tight for a moment. "Definitely aren't."

She squirmed. He liked it. He ignored it.

"No, and I never claimed I was him. I'm just using him as an example. Anyhow, according to the story, he used to play an instrument and the animals would obey him."

"Are you saying you control animals? With what, that weird humming sound?" He couldn't stem his incredulity. It sounded farfetched when said aloud, and yet, he couldn't help but recall the mesmerized state of the creatures crowding that clearing.

"I guess it's what I do, in a sense. It's a little more complicated than that, but you get the general idea."

His brow wrinkled as he had a thought. "In the story, didn't the piper dude end up leading the children away with his music?"

"If this is your way of asking if I can do it to humans or shifters, then the answer is no. Mostly."

"What do you mean, mostly?"

Again with the shrug and the boob shift against him, which really was tempting him to loosen his grip so he could cup.

Randy wolf. *Behave!*

"While animals seem to obey with fairly little trouble, those with a developed mind can resist. They have a strong sense of free will. I cannot compel them. But if I'm in extreme danger, and they're not strong minded enough…"

He grasped where she was going and finished. "Then sometimes your mind control thing works."

Her head bobbed.

He whistled. "You are one dangerous chick."

"I suppose."

"You're also in cahoots with the enemy." He stated it with confidence. It seemed obvious given the evidence. Their town had been plagued in all the recent attacks by wild creatures. Wolves, even jackrabbits and some other creatures, had joined shapeshifters in nipping at Kodiak Point. At the time, they'd wondered at the strange behavior of the wildlife. Now he had an answer, make that a culprit.

Wait until Reid and the others find out. They'll shit kittens.

Telling, though, would have to wait until he

escaped.

"I do not do *his* bidding willingly." How vehemently she said it.

"I didn't see you trying to escape too hard when I came across you." Oh say it like it was, when he'd foolishly walked right into the obvious trap.

"I've spent years trying to escape. Take a look around and tell me how well that's worked."

Her sarcasm amused him.

Not acceptable. She didn't grasp the situation obviously. Prisoner or not, he was in charge, and he had to remain firm.

I'm the boss. I'm the one with her life in my hands.

He tightened his grip. "How do I know you're telling the truth? For all I know this is yet another trap."

"A trap? How?"

"Oh please. It's so obvious. You pretending you're all sweet and innocent, little miss victim stuck in the cage with the captured wolf, when in reality you're trying to soften me up so you can siphon me for information. I'll tell you right now, honey, you can tempt me with your feminine wiles, you can attempt to seduce me with your body, but I'll never crack." But he really hoped she'd try her damnedest.

She shook, a tremble of her upper body that transferred to his. He shifted. Again, she shuddered, and she made a low noise, a choked sound that was…laughter?

Mirth rocked her body. Chuckles bubbled forth in a musical wave of sound.

"You'll have to fill me in, sweetheart, because I'm not getting the joke."

In between giggles, she managed to gasp, "I'm laughing at your assumption. Or, rather, your hope that they placed me in this cage to play the part of sexy siren. On the contrary, sir wolf, I am surprised they've even allowed you to touch me. I am the master's prized pet and prisoner. This cage you see with the pallet and the books is my home. It is you who has been put in here with me. I just don't know why. I thought for sure to hear your screams by now. The ones *he* captures usually don't last long."

The information that spilled from her took a long blink to process. One fact stood out. This was her home.

His grip on her loosened, and he allowed her to step away. Although, he almost grabbed her back. She truly did fit too well against him.

He let his gaze roam the space. At ten by ten, it wasn't large, barely a small bedroom, but one framed in bars on three sides and a cinder block wall for the fourth. Although, he'd already tasted the silver on the bars facing the stairs, he still brushed a finger along all of them, the sizzling burn of each testifying that it wasn't just a few that bore the burning taint.

He moved his glance to what the cage held. A mound of blankets atop an air mattress took up part of the floor. He crouched by the bed. A simple inhalation brought him her rich scent. Those were her sheets. But someone could have planted them in here for authenticity.

Against the stone wall sat a toilet and, beside it, a chipped white porcelain sink, the cheap faucet rusted with time and calcium deposits. There was only one more thing of note in the cage—if one ignored the woman watching his inspection with an amused gaze. Stacked in messy piles were books, tawdry books. Books with shirtless men grasping women with half-awake visages, spilling bosoms, and wind-blown locks.

"You read that?" His remark might have emerged a tad dismissive because she took a defensive, yet stubborn, tone when she replied.

Chin angled, she said, "Yes, I read *that*. It's called romance."

"Romance?" He snorted. "Let's call it what it is. You read dirty books."

The glare she shot him was probably meant to cow, but damn if she didn't look hotter.

"What is it with men and their judgmental ways? It's a romance book, as in a story about a man and a woman who have some type of adventure, fall in love, and end up living happily ever after."

"And have sex."

Despite her tanned skin, her cheeks still pinked. "Yes, they have intimate relations. But it's not the sole focus of the book. And why am I defending my reading material to you? It's none of your business what I like to read."

"You're right. It's not. I just thought it was interesting." Although not as interesting as the fact that when she planted her hands on her hips she outlined a shapely hourglass figure.

I knew it. Unfortunately, knowing didn't lessen her allure but rather made it worse.

"If you're done judging me, maybe I should ask what you're doing in *my* room?"

He shrugged. "The hell if I know. I woke with this fucking zap collar just minutes before you got here. I haven't talked to anyone yet." Nor killed anyone. He was totally going soft. Here he was discoursing with a woman when he should be hunting for a way out.

The answer to his presence came from a speaker strung on a wire atop their cage. And look at that. There was a camera beside it! Someone was playing Peeping Tom.

He cranked his middle finger and smiled at the lens.

"That's mature," she muttered.

You ain't seen nothing yet.

A synthesized voice emerged from the plastic speaker. "I see you've met your new roommate, my pet."

Of all the degrading things to call a Lycan. "Don't call me pet," Brody growled, his fists clenched at his side.

The woman snorted. "Um, sorry to break it to you, Mr. World Revolves Him, but he's talking to me. I'm"—she made a face—"his pet."

"First off, while you are correct that the world does orbit around my greatness," a world that barely slid by his modesty, "my actual name is—"

"Brody Johnson," said the robotic voice from the speaker. "Retired soldier and currently second-in-command to Reid, alpha at Kodiak Point. During your military days, you served under Sergeant Carson. On your last mission, several years ago now, you were captured by insurgents during a routine area sweep. You spent the next eight months in captivity until your escape, where you killed the leader and burned down three-quarters of the camp. You managed to rescue at the same time, three others, Reid, Boris, and Kyle. Poor Gene, he got to spend another year in that place. No wonder he felt so abandoned."

As the faceless voice recited pivotal parts of his life, a chill swept Brody. "Who is this? And how do you know so much about me?" Brody fought to keep his emotions in check, but the more he heard, the more he realized just how targeted the ambush of him was. Some of the information was classified. How the hell did the speaker find so much out?

"I know everything."

Someone didn't suffer from self-esteem issues. "Did you know I'm going to kill you?" Bluffing, one of the most powerful tools a man could sometimes wield.

Unless someone called it. A mechanical laughter did not reassure. "You are welcome to try. It wouldn't be the first attempt. But I'll warn you right now, death doesn't want me."

"Death wants everyone." Especially if handed to the reaper by one determined wolf. "So who are you anyhow?" Gathering clues was the key to taking down an enemy.

"You may call me master."

Forget holding in his snicker. "Good luck with that, buddy. I'm no one's slave."

"You say that now, but..." The voice trailed off. Not that Brody would have heard much as his teeth began to vibrate.

Thud.

The shock of the collar blasted through him, and he writhed like a worm on hot pavement. So much for keeping better control the second time.

When the current cut off, he took a moment to clear his senses.

Bait made a tsking sound. "You really shouldn't antagonize him."

"No kidding. He must really have a small dick to need a—"

Ouch! Brody could practically feel his hair stand on end with the newest round, and was that a burning smell? At least this time, he managed, if barely, to keep his eyes open and thus saw as Bait tossed her hair back and glared defiantly at the camera.

Oh god, she wasn't going to beg for mercy, was she? His man card would get revoked for sure.

No, she had more pressing concerns than his possible demise by electrocution. "If you're going to kill him, could you please do it somewhere else? And where's my chocolate?"

Her request didn't exactly make him feel all warm and fuzzy, but it did give him the oomph needed to say, "Thanks for your sympathy. You have no idea how this hurts."

"Don't I?"

She grabbed her hair in a fist and, with her free hand, yanked at the neckline of her gown to show a collar ringing her neck, a twin to his own.

No wonder she behaved. If he could barely keep from screaming at the pain, how must it be for her?

He shook his head in disbelief. "Dude isn't just small-dicked. He's so weak he tortures women, too."

Bad news. Little dick flipped on the juice. Good news, Brody was starting to get used to the shock. Kind of. His tongue no longer flopped out of his mouth.

When he'd stopped doing the jiggle, he opened his eyes to see a concerned mauve gaze hovering over him. "Stings, eh?"

"Just a little," he said with a grimace as he rose from his ignoble kneeling position.

Robot voice interrupted. "How nice to see you both bonding. It will make the reason I've brought you together easier. Pet, meet the man who will father upon you a child."

Brody had barely digested the words before she was yelling. "Oh, hell no. You will not whore me out. Remember what happened to the last men you sent to try. I hear they never did find all the body parts."

Say what? Brody sought to connect all the dots, but the picture that emerged as the conversation unfolded didn't result in anything pleasant.

"Those previous attempts were mistakes. I sent in minions to do the job of a warrior. You won't find this man so easy to break."

"Don't count on it," she muttered. "If it didn't work with them, don't think for one second it will happen with him. I won't have sex with him."

Funny how she denied the faceless one's demand, and yet Brody could hear her racing heart, sense the flush on her skin. It seemed the idea of fucking him wasn't entirely without appeal, despite her more than vehement claim to the contrary.

Speaking of which, did she have to be so vehement?

I'm a good-looking guy. Most women would jump at the chance to pounce my bones.

"You say that, and yet both know you will, in the end, do as you're told. You should thank me, pet, for my choice. You see, Brody isn't like the others I sent to you. I chose him specially because of his strength."

"I won't let him rape me."

Excuse me? Brody held out his hands in a timeout gesture. "Slow down there, sweetheart. Who said anything about forcing you? I would never do that."

"You say that now." She stared pointedly at his collar.

He frowned. The woman thought a little pain would get him to do something so vile? She'd soon learn. Brody wasn't one to cave to torture.

But she might.

Brody knew the moment a zap was sent to her collar. Her eyes widened, and he could practically feel the zing of electricity. Yet she didn't utter a sound. Nor did she drop to her knees. Or do anything at all to show she was being electrocuted.

He must have her on a lower setting.

But still, it had to smart. When it ended, her eyes took on a dark glow, a simmering storm that radiated from every tense muscle in her body. Totally hot.

Mr. Roboto wasn't quite done yapping. "Think upon it, pet. Then act. You know, in the end, you will do as I wish. What other choice do you have?"

"You might think you control my choices, but I'll find a way to thwart you," she muttered darkly.

"You can try. But as you have all the other times, you'll fail." With those parting words, the speaker went silent, even the static of the open mike ceasing. But Brody remained all too aware of the watching camera.

What an interesting conversation, which, if he took at face value, made her a prisoner of this dude with visions of grandeur. He also had a reason as to why they'd chosen him, so he could play stud.

Seriously? In this day and age of sperm banks, why go through the trouble of kidnapping someone for sex?

Not just anyone though, a wolf. So maybe not so farfetched after all. And really, could anyone dispute the choice? Brody was, after all, a fine male specimen.

One who liked to live dangerously. "So, *pet,*

is this where you burst into tears and beg me to take you so we don't get punished?"

"You pig."

"It's wolf, pet."

His breath emerged in an oomph as she slugged him in the gut. Bait might possess a soft body, but she knew just where to hit a man.

"What was that for?" he exclaimed.

"Don't call me that. Don't ever call me that," she practically shouted. Her lips pursed. "It's what *he* calls me. But I have a name. It's Layla. L-a-y-la." She enunciated each letter slowly.

I think I just got told. He didn't apologize, but he did offer an olive branch. "I'm Brody."

She rolled her eyes. "I already know."

"Yeah, but that was douchebag introducing us. Now I'm doing it. Truce?" He held out his hand, sincere in his offer. Until he knew what was going on, she remained his best bet at getting answers and maybe even discovering the key to his escape.

And Sarge always taught us to keep our enemies close.

Without warning, the lights went out.

"What now?" he asked.

"Our cue to go to bed."

"But we just got up."

"Maybe you did, but I didn't. I got to enjoy a three-hour snowmobile ride. Then eight hours in the back of a truck with you snoring."

"I do not snore."

"Then there is something seriously wrong with you."

"You know, Bait, for a woman who's expected to bed me, you're not being very nice."

"And you're supposed to be strong. I'd say we're both disappointed."

She might not see it in the dark, but yeah, his jaw dropped. What a mouthy woman. "Are you always this rude?"

"Only when inspired. Listen. I'm sure you're a very nice guy on the outside. But in here, with me, you're just another problem I need to worry about."

"I'm not sure I appreciate your implication."

"I'm sorry, imply? Let me clear that up for you. I. Do. Not. Trust. You. And it's nothing you've done, but escape thirty-six taught me to never put my faith in anyone else. Actually escape twenty-one did too, but thirty-six is the one that really hurt."

He zeroed in on an interesting clue. "Escape thirty-six?"

"Yes. You noted earlier that I didn't seem to fight my fate. I did in the past. But, after a while, especially when you constantly fail, you learn which battles to wage and which to ignore. With you, no matter the act you put on, I can't for a minute believe it. It wouldn't be the first time *he* tried to fool me."

Or was she pulling one over Brody? Was this a case of double misdirection? By pretending she didn't trust him, did she think he'd think he could trust her? Good grief, say that aloud fast, five times.

"Believe what you will, but I'm not working for your dude. Nor do I harm women."

"All right then. Good night."

"Good night? You're going to sleep?"

"Yes and so should you. Who knows what we'll have to deal with tomorrow."

"I'm not sleeping." As if. He'd stay crouched where he was, thank you very much. A soldier never let the enemy take him by surprise.

"Whatever. You'll regret it in the morning."

He heard the rustle of blankets as she settled herself. Quiet descended except for the occasional pipe rattling as a toilet flushed or water ran upstairs. There were pops and creaks of a house settling. The skitter of little feet?

The idea of creeping rats, filthy things, made him eye the darkness with suspicion. It also made him blurt, "I know why you want me to sleep so bad."

"Yes. I have a horrible ulterior motive. It's called seeing you rested."

"Ha. You want me to sleep so that you can use your power to call some of your furry minions."

"Minions? I like that. It's got a certain ring."

"So you don't deny it?"

"Deny what?"

"The fact you're planning to use your minions."

"Let's say, I'm biting, what am I having these furry minions do exactly?"

Given Brody spent a lot of time in prisons, not all of them with safety standards, he'd seen first-hand the disturbing kind of damage rodents could inflict. "Do? I don't know. Chew my face off. Sever an artery."

"Ooh, gouge the eyeballs from your head." She laughed. "Or, or, I know, how about they climb into your mouth and then claw their way through your stomach?"

She couldn't do that, could she? He clamped his lips tight and grimaced. "Now you're just being gross."

"Nope, I'm mocking you because you're an idiot."

This conversation was not going at all how planned. She was supposed to answer his questions, not ridicule him. He tried to veer this conversation back on track. "Are you denying you could make them do it?"

"No, but I wouldn't waste rats, or any other animals I could call, on you."

"Why? Am I not good enough?" He said it and then realized how it sounded.

"You're not worth the effort or waste of resource. I mean, you're stuck in here with me. Why kill you when I could use those minions to kill the guards?"

"You can do that with rats?"

"A second ago you were convinced I could."

Well, only half seriously. After all, come on, he was a wolf, like he'd let some rodents take him out. "If you can do it, then prove it."

"Do what? Kill the guards? I can't."

"Why not? I thought you just said you

could."

"Sure, if there were any rodents nearby. There's nothing left for me to use in a pretty large radius except for a few insects and spiders."

"Why should I believe you?"

"You're right, you shouldn't. Good night. Sweet dreams. Don't let the bed bugs bite." Her giggle didn't reassure at all.

Good night? As if he'd sleep. If there was one thing he'd learned in that tropical prison he'd spent two weeks in was the rats weren't picky when it came to food. And they liked bare toes.

He still had a hard time sleeping without his boots on. Unbidden, his naked feet shuffled closer together, and he squatted lower on them, alert to even the slightest tickle of an approaching rodent invasion.

When several minutes went by with nothing spoken, he thought about striking up another conversation, but judging by the evenness of her breath, she slept.

So much for her not trusting me. Or was this a case of not fearing?

Maybe I should join Kyle in his quest to restore his bad-ass reputation.

Chapter Four

Layla couldn't help but giggle after her jest about bed bugs. She was only half kidding. She could get them to bite, just not easily. Their tiny flickers of existence were hard to hold and control. But even if she used a bedbug one at a time, she could still cause damage. There was just one problem. There were none left.

Apart from a few small spiders, the only living creature in proximity was a man. A wolf. A threat to her body if the master was serious about him mating with her.

Such a dangerous cellmate, especially since if he made an attempt to seduce she wasn't sure she'd resist.

The cage had seemed small before when it held just her. Add in a six-foot-plus man who wore only jeans, a sculpted torso, and shaggy, streaked dark brown and blond hair? It was stifling and warm.

Oh *so* warm.

The flush of it tingled along her nerve endings. Hyper aware of him, and every nuance of his presence, only served to deepen the sensation.

Despite her inexperience, she knew what it

meant.

Desire throbbed between her legs, incited by need and lusty thoughts for the man sharing her space. The unexpected attraction might have proved easier to deal with if not for the master's twisted demand. *He wants me to allow this stranger to bed me.* The handsome, virile man who prowled their confined space, the grace of his stealthy perusal fascinating to watch. It did nothing to diminish the heat within her.

How easy to allow herself to give in to her body's curiosity.

But in doing so, she would be willingly doing something the master wanted.

Help him?

Ha. Never. Which meant she would have to do anything she could to ensure she remained chaste. She would fight, like she always did. She might lose, but she would never give in easily.

That was assuming she had to fend off the wolf. The master's command seemed to have not mattered an iota to Brody. He showed not even the slightest interest in her. Which, in an odd twist, miffed her.

He could pretend, at least, a little interest.

And with that thought, she set her mini minion with eight legs to spy on him where he crouched and let herself sleep. She knew better than to deprive herself.

When she awoke the next day, the sudden glare of the lights illuminating a shocking wake-up call, she noted that he'd indeed spent the night crouched, watching and waiting.

"Morning," she said as she stretched.

Through the hank of hair on his forehead, he perused her. He grunted in reply.

"Aren't you a ray of sunshine?" she said, rolling free of her blankets to stand.

"Being a prisoner will do that to a man."

"Great. Not only am I stuck with you for the moment, but you're a grumpy puss."

"Wolf."

"Whatever. Mind plugging your ears while I attend to business."

"You're going to pee?" He sounded so shocked.

"Yes. And brush my teeth. Is that a problem?"

"But I'm here."

"So I noticed. Hence the request."

"Woman don't pee around men."

How she wished that were true. "I have to go, and I see no reason to hold it in to protect your delicate sensibilities."

"Delicate?"

"Yes, delicate. This is not a five-star hotel. Heck, on the scale of prisons, I don't know if it even ranks a one. Which means, no walls, which means you get to hear and see it all. So get used to it. If it's any consolation, I imagine you will have to tinkle as well at some point. I promise to not watch when you do."

"I'll escape before then."

As Layla sat on the throne, her cheeks burning despite her brave words, she murmured, "Good luck with that."

He'd thankfully already averted his gaze and now clapped his hands over his ears as she took care of her pressing bladder. He even hummed. She wondered what he'd do when her second order of business decided it needed tending. She'd gotten used to a lack of privacy over the years, but there was ugly, leering guards and cameras, and then there was handsome hunk in a cage with her.

Nothing screamed romance like seeing and hearing a woman pee.

Good thing I'm not planning seduction then.

Once she brushed her teeth, she returned to sit cross-legged on her bed. As if that were a sign, he finally rose to his feet and did his own version of a morning stretch.

She should have looked away. Pretended interest in a wall.

Yeah, that didn't happen.

One glimpse of rippling flesh as he pulled his arms over his head, to the front, back, and she was mesmerized.

"Good thing there's no flies left, or you'd catch some," he remarked as he caught her staring.

She snapped her mouth shut. "Sorry. As you might have noticed, the entertainment level is kind of low, so anything new is kind of fascinating. Even you." She tried to make it sound disparaging, but he smirked, too easily reading the lie.

"So what do you do all day?" he asked, still stretching his limbs.

"Depends on if the master is having a villain day or not."

"A villain what?"

"Some days, the master likes to take me out of the cage, and he'll have me set a group of animals on a task. Usually something nefarious. I call those villain days."

"And when you're not on a task for him?"

She shrugged. "Not much. I read. Insult the guards. Plot escape."

His gaze caught hers. "Plot? What about executing an escape?"

"Like I've said. I've tried. So far, that hasn't worked out so well for me." Or else she wouldn't be at number fifty-seven.

"Then perhaps it's a good thing we've been placed together."

Before she could reply, the sound of feet stomping down the stairs caught their attention. Breakfast time.

Familiar with the routine, Layla didn't bother moving from her bed, but Brody did. He loomed a few inches from the bars.

"Move back, dog," said the tall, skinny one, his usual sneer stretching his thin lips.

"And if I don't?" Still belligerent.

Layla held in a sigh as Brody was sent to his knees, his collar activated, long enough for the guard to shove the MRE rations through the bars.

The silver foil packet didn't excite her. She now knew why astronauts were so skinny. Their food sucked.

As she ate the uninspiring mash of fake eggs, chunks of simulated bacon, and other factory-created ingredients thrown together to make an unappetizing scrambled mess, she noted

Brody didn't bother with his. He seemed more intent on other things this morning.

With his broad back turned—displaying even more of his muscular upper body—he paced the outline of the cage, examining it from the floor where the bars sank in to cement to the ceiling where those same bars were welded across the top. An escape-proof prison.

And home sweet home.

"You can't get out," she stated.

He didn't bother to turn to face her as he replied. "Perhaps you can't. But every prison has a flaw. It's just a matter of finding it."

"You speak from experience?"

"I do actually." He peered over his shoulder at her from his crouched position by the sink. Hair flopped over his brow while more of it stuck out wildly, mussed and beckoning fingers to comb through it. So sexy.

She diverted her thoughts with another mouthful of icky mush. When he didn't elaborate on his experience, she asked, "Why were you in prison?"

"Wrong place. Wrong time. Happens a lot in my line of work."

"Did you escape, or were you rescued?"

"Most of the time I escaped. Usually within days or weeks. There was only one prison that took me a while. My captor in that case was real good at keeping my kind chained. But in the end, he couldn't hold me, or my brothers."

"Your whole family was there?"

"Military brothers is what I should have

said. I consider them family. Once you've stared down death with a guy, then charged at it snarling, you kind of forge a bond. That type of thing sticks with you. It's a thing that goes beyond friendship."

"I wouldn't know. I'm always alone."

"Always?"

The conversation veered uncomfortably close to a place she preferred not to visit. In order to remain positive and strong, there were certain emotions she preferred not to examine too closely. Loneliness was one of them. She yanked the direction of their conversation back to what he was doing, which was lifting her bedding as she washed her hands at the sink. He checked the floor beneath it.

"It's all concrete. No hidden trap doors. I told you, I've looked and found nothing. But if you want to waste some time, suit yourself," she said as she dried her hands on her gown.

No reply as he finished his examination of the cell. He also ignored her, not once glancing her way, which for some reason needled.

I should be happy he's ignoring me. After all, she didn't want to have to fend against any advances, or have him accuse her of working voluntarily for the master.

So ignoring was good.

No, it's not. She'd not had this much interaction with someone in ages.

He spun suddenly and, brows drawn, asked, "How come you can't order the guards to let you go? Because, let's be honest here, Joe Seal and Tom Walrus aren't the sharpest tools in the shed.

You said your power works in extreme situations against the weak. Wouldn't this count?"

If the situation were less serious, she might have giggled at his names of the morning shift guards. "It's not life or death. So no. It doesn't. And when I manage to convince one to help me out of the goodness of their heart, they end up dying."

"Dying how?"

She wrinkled her nose. "It's kind of gruesome. They all carry around some kind of poison in their tooth. Somehow, I don't know how, as soon as they so much as think of releasing me, crunch, they pop the pill, and seconds later they're foaming at the mouth and hitting the ground."

"That is unusual. And you're not the one compelling them to do it?"

She shook her head.

"Okay, then here's another question. If you can get them to self destruct by begging them to set you free, why not decimate his army and get out of here?" He didn't ask in jest, but all seriousness.

She saw no harm in answering. He'd soon learn the master had all the bases covered, which was why she'd been working on escape fifty-seven for so long now. "He usually never sends in more than a few at a time, and each time I accidentally cause their demise, I go days without food or water. Since starving myself serves no purpose, I stopped."

She'd tried only a few times because even if

they were abetting in holding her prisoner, it wasn't the lackeys' fault they couldn't escape the clutches of the psycho master.

"Deprivation. A tool of a true sadist," Brody muttered. "Interesting."

For some reason his cool analysis angered her. "How is that interesting?" she snapped. "Try more like horrifying. The master is a sick psycho who kidnapped me a few years ago, killed my father, and holds me prisoner. Oh and now wants to impregnate me by a stranger, to do who knows what to my baby. My tale is a lot of things, but interesting isn't one of them." She practically yelled the last part at him, angry at his casual dismissal of the situation—*my life*.

"Calm down, sweetheart. I didn't mean to diss your treatment. I'm just reconnoitering. As I find out more and more, I'm able to build a profile of this master person. Know thine enemy. Best piece of advice ever."

Layla knew the enemy, but had yet to see how that helped her. "All I know is he needs to die." Straight and to the point. Why bother hiding it? The master might watch and listen—when she didn't fuck with his spy equipment—but he already knew of her hatred.

"Never doubt I'm working on his demise. What does he look like by the way? No one we've talked to ever seems to have a clear recollection."

The mystery question. "No one remembers because he doesn't allow it. Most of the time, he wears a hood over his head. No one ever sees his face. And if anyone has, they're not talking. I'm not sure what magic he has, but whatever it is, part of it involves people being unable to describe him."

"Even you?"

"Even me." Nor could she control the master at all, even when he managed to terrify her. Going at the master's mind was like hitting a steel wall. Impenetrable. But she still liked to hammer at it just to irritate him.

"How long have you been his prisoner?"

"A while. And before him, there were others."

"Others?" His query held an inquisitive note.

"Oh yes. I've spent quite a few years of my life as somebody's property. He's just the newest and longest-running master I've ever had. The ones who survived owning me ended up selling me because I proved difficult."

"Couldn't you escape?"

She rolled her eyes. "I did. Many times. Freedom doesn't last long when you wear a tracker."

"You've been chipped?"

She nodded.

"Damn." His eyes held a measure of pity, and she turned away.

Keep the pity for someone else. Yes, her life, make that un-life, sucked, but giving up would never make it better. Only by trying could she keep hope alive. "It's made escapes more of a challenge."

"Where is it?"

"Somewhere on my back I assume. I've

checked every inch of my front and sides. There's nothing there." She'd presented the guards with quite the scene as she disrobed a body part at a time, peering at her skin in the harsh light from the UV lights bolted to the ceiling.

She'd examined every inch of flesh, more than once, but never saw even a single suspicious speck. Nor did she find a trace of a scar.

"What's the farthest you ever made it once you did slip his grasp?"

"More like longest is what you should ask. My record in the last three years was three days and eleven hours." Eighty-three hours of adrenaline as she ran and evaded bounty hunters sicced to her trail. Ever since the master who wanted her to make his personal zoo pets do stupid circus tricks, she was always watched. Always followed. And she never escaped for long. Someone was always on her trail as soon as she fled, and they made sure she never got too far.

And now she couldn't escape at all, although she'd done her damnedest in the year since she became the master's pet. A busy year. Yet, no matter how she fought, how many she killed, or how well she plotted, she remained stuck in her cage.

The worse part? The master laughed at her attempts to escape, and then he punished her.

But she didn't tell all this to Brody. Divulging her secrets never came to any good.

"That tracker needs to come out," he stated.

"Well duh." She rolled her eyes. "Got a

knife and some bandages and a way to not have the guards zap us like bugs as soon as you try?"

"Good points. We'll have to hold off until I've fully formulated a plan."

Such hope. She could almost admire it. "You really think you can escape?"

"It's not a matter of can. I will. And when I do…" He grinned. "Be ready."

The smile he sported blazed and totally stole her breath. So handsome and, at the same time, so crazy. What a shame. She knew Brody had to possess a flaw. It appeared optimism in the face of bad odds was one of them.

"Why is it you don't seem too upset you got dumped here?" Actually, if she were honest, the more Brody seemed to examine their impossible situation, the more energized he became.

"Why would I be upset? Danger. Adventure. A puzzle to solve. Plus, I got to meet you." He winked and shot her a sensual smile.

She blinked. *Is he seriously flirting with me?* Like hell. "That is the corniest thing I've ever heard."

"It's true. If I'm going to be captured and spend time in a cell, then what better way than with a beautiful woman?"

Astonishment aside, she couldn't help a spurt of pleasure at his compliment. Then his ploy became clear, and she glared. "I get it now. You're not really a prisoner. This is all part of a ploy from you accosting me in the clearing to your whole pretend capture. They were all devised plots to make me believe you were a prisoner so I'd feel a bond with you, and then, when you turn your charm on the poor, lonely girl, I'm supposed to melt into a little pile of goo that you could use at your whim."

"Are you done? Because, wow, that is the most confusing, and utterly false, thing I've ever heard. I don't work for that douchebag. And if I tell a woman she's pretty, then it's because she is."

She frowned. "You mean you were actually flirting?"

"Hell yeah I was. I mean, we're in a fucking cage. Until I find a way out, we gotta live together. It might help if we became friends."

Friends? What an odd concept?

One she suddenly longed for desperately.

Chapter Five

Apparently, Brody had poured on too much of the charm and the woman caught on. It had been worth a try, especially once it occurred to him that softening Layla toward him would maybe get her to reveal secrets, secrets she didn't mean to. Anything that might indicate if she was playing him for a fool because, really, the more she told of her story, the more he had to wonder if she pulled his paw.

Prisoner for years? Surely not.

The beautiful woman with the captivating gaze and luscious body appeared anything but a cowed victim. She held pride. Determination. She didn't seem like someone who'd spent years in custody.

But what about the cage, and the collar?

Were they props for her story? Was this whole thing a ploy to get him to spill his guts or to garner sympathy so he'd feel drawn to her?

As if I need help in that department.

Their tight quarters made it impossible to avoid her presence. Especially her scent.

It wrapped around him in a perfumed gossamer. It roused his wild side. Made it pace.

Hunger. Not to eat. But for more.

Want more of her scent. Want to rub against her. Mate her. Bite her…

Slap. It wasn't a physical one, but a mental one. Brody reeled his irrational wolf back in line.

Dude, we are not doing any of those things. For the moment, she is a civilian, and a possible enemy. We know the rules. Observe. Seek out. And, if needed, destroy.

Currently, Layla fell under the observe column. He'd watch, take notes, and, at the same time, befriend her. Right now, she appeared just as suspicious of him as he was of her. If she told the truth about her situation, then she could prove a valuable ally.

She tells the truth.

His beast seemed so certain, but Brody didn't think it would hurt to gather more Intel. In order to do that, he needed to get closer so she relaxed around him and divulged all her secrets— such as what hid under that gown.

No.

He was not flirting with her to get her to shed her clothes.

Although, he wouldn't argue if she did. He also probably wouldn't be able to help himself.

Alas, she did not strip. She dove into her pile of blankets and put even more fabric between them.

A shame.

She also seemed intent on ignoring him, burying her nose in one of her tawdry romance novels.

Hmph. Wasting her time with a cardboard

hero when she had the real thing within reach.

No matter. He had more pressing things to do, such as devising a plan of action.

Despite his first perusal, Brody spent some more time examining their prison. How the bars met the floor. The thickness of the welds at the top. He tried thrusting a hand through the tight silver bars to palpate the lock but hissed as the silver scored his skin and, in the end, learned nothing, other than burnt hair stank.

At least singed hair hurt less than a wax strip down the middle of his somewhat furred chest, yanked by a sadistic polar bear. Fucking Gene.

Thinking of Gene made him wonder how the attack on Kodiak Point had turned out. *Did they prevail? Were there casualties?*

And did his disappearance garner any notice?

With the chaos of attack, it would take some time for them to decipher the events and realize he never made it back to town. If too much time passed, would they even find his trail in the woods and discover his fate?

Probably not, which meant he was on his own. A solo mission.

For some reason that made him think of Kyle, whose personality quirk—which shrinks insisted on calling a disorder—resulted in him going through life in terms of missions.

My mission? Get my ass out of here. And maybe bring the girl.

Who was he kidding about maybe? Layla

was coming with him.

On the surface, he labeled her as a person of interest, someone that Reid would want to meet. But, if Brody dug a little deeper into his intentions, the man—and, yes, his pesky wolf—also wanted to rescue her from this sad fate. To see her eyes shine with appreciation and bask in the warmth of her thanks—naked.

No. Not naked.

He really needed to get his shit together and stop thinking of her as an attractive woman. He tried. He ignored her as best he could, only to get miffed when she paid him not the slightest bit of attention. Not once did he catch her staring.

Must be a good book.

As if words on paper could compare to the real thing. *But what if she's never experienced anything more than words?* As a captive, her options for socialization, and romance, were limited.

She could very well be innocent. The concept almost dropped him to his knees.

We could teach her.

Oh, now didn't that bring to mind a bunch of possibilities? Fantasies he quickly squashed.

For now he needed to focus on spotting a weakness. None appeared, but he didn't give up hope. He'd keep observing.

The guards re-appeared at one point during the day—who knew what time? Without windows and any measure of daylight, he couldn't have said how much time passed. He did know the guards took sadistic pleasure with zapping him into submission so they could toss more unpalatable crap in their cage. Ugh. MREs. He'd have preferred a can of dog food. Some at least had a palatable gravy.

But food was food. Eventually, he did cave and eat some of the mush because he needed to keep his strength up. Who knew how long he'd spend in this cage until he found a crack in the defense?

With the cage thoroughly explored, it was time to question Layla on her knowledge of what lay beyond the bars. What could he expect at the top of the stairs? How many men were there usually? He'd counted six individuals so far. What kind of weapons did they bear?

And where the fuck were they being held? If he got his paws on a phone, he'd call Reid, or Boris, someone to relay his situation to. It would vastly help to have a general idea of his location.

Forget asking, though, as Layla, without a word to him, had fallen fast asleep in her nest of blankets.

How angelic she appeared in repose. Her dark lashes touching the tops of her cheeks. Her lips soft and inviting. Her hair fanned out around her head.

He couldn't stop staring at her. It creeped him out, but he couldn't help himself. She drew his eyes and thoughts. *I am a man obsessed.* Or possessed. Did she have some kind of unknown magic that made him feel this way?

The lights went out so abruptly he saw spots. He blinked at the darkness in an effort to dispel them.

So much for a goodnight warning.

No more investigating—or eyeballing Layla—for the moment. In the pitch-black, he'd more than likely burn himself on the silver bars if he blundered around. He hunkered down to the floor, this time sitting in a Lotus position. The chill of the concrete seeped immediately through the fabric of his jeans.

Brrr.

This wouldn't do. Not for a second night in a row. *I need a blanket.* He turned his head in the darkness, toward Bait. There were blankets promising warmth just a few feet away, more than enough for two—especially if they shared.

The idea locked into place, and without a second thought, he was in motion. Cautiously, on hands and knees, he crept in the darkness until he hit the mound of sheets. Further groping located a curvy shape under them. Layla didn't move.

He tugged at the blankets until he held up an edge and could ease into their warm embrace. The squashy air mattress provided a little cushion for his frame, but best of all, it cut the chill of the floor. But what truly heated him was her.

Entering her intimate sleeping space meant inhaling her with every breath. Sensing her. Wanting her.

He blamed it on the small blankets for why he nestled close to her, his body spooning around the curve of her buttocks, fitting against him with maddening perfection. His cock took notice. Every inch of him did actually.

His jeans chafed the erection he couldn't

stop, rubbing against the rough fabric. No underwear because he'd chosen to go commando, knowing all too well how ridiculous a shifter could look if he did a sudden morph and still sported his underwear.

Poor Munroe, he never did live down the time he went barreling after some enemy soldiers in white jockeys. He was forever Wedge.

If Brody were alone, he would have peeled the denim. Yet he'd kept the single layer of clothing, despite his discomfort, to preserve his modesty.

Screech.

Brakes applied, and he reversed.

Wait a second? Nudity didn't bother him. He liked to let his skin breath, and it truly was more comfortable to shift in the nude. *Holy moon goddess, don't tell me I kept the pants on to preserve her modesty?*

Like Hell. That wouldn't do at all. He should take them off.

And tempt her into seducing you.

No. He didn't want seduction. Just a chance to let Johnson breathe. Poor guy was stifled. He also had some oxygen-deprived ideas.

Sleeping with Bait might buy time and get some answers about this master dude who is holding you prisoner.

Getting Intel was a valid reason for seduction, but that wasn't why he snapped the button fly on his jeans. He already had the best reason to shimmy out of his pants because, if he didn't, they were going to rub his poor dick raw. His denuding movements, while quick, did not pass unnoticed.

"What are you doing?" Said slowly and with a querying note at the end.

"Getting naked." And for those who wondered? Yeah, he said it with a naughty, wolfish grin.

She, however, couldn't see it, nor did she react too well at the words. "For what purpose?"

He could have screwed with her and told her it would ease the amount of undressing needed for the passionate sex they were about to have. However, given the tenseness of the tightly spoken question, he thought it best to not antagonize her further.

"I'm getting naked to sleep."

"With me?"

"I don't see another bed. So I guess we'll have to *share*." And yes, he did let the implication that he meant something more infuse his words. A man had to have some kind of fun.

She, however, didn't find it entertaining, or appealing. "Oh no you don't," she muttered. She went into motion, throwing back the covers, but before she could rise, he clamped his arm around her waist and tugged her back against him.

"You're not going anywhere, sweetheart." Not just because he was insulted at her vehement rebuff of him but because now was the perfect time to try and forge some trust. Show her he meant her no harm.

"Let me go."

He thought about it while she thrashed and struggled. She called him names, some in languages he couldn't understand but deciphered given their vehemence. When she finally calmed her failed attempts to escape, he said, "Done?" He hoped not because he quite enjoyed the feel of her in his arms and against him.

"You are a jerk."

"Why? Because I won't let you stumble around in the dark?"

"I know this cage better than I know you. I'd have no problem."

"It's cold, and there's only one bed."

"I'm well aware of that and the fact you seem to think you can use it. And me. I won't allow it."

"You seem to have gotten the wrong impression, sweetheart. I didn't get nude for you. I did it because it's more bloody comfortable. Have you ever slept in jeans? The fabric chafes, especially against my more manly parts. Johnson needed fresh air."

"Johnson?"

"Yeah, Johnson. It's what I call *it*."

"You named your penis?"

He cringed. "Ack, woman. Don't use that word."

"What word? Penis?"

He growled.

"Penis. Penis. Penis."

He growled louder.

She laughed. "I can't believe you're offended by the word. I mean, haven't I heard you use the word fuck?"

"A perfectly acceptable verb, pronoun, and

adjective."

"And penis is the accepted name for your man parts."

He almost flinched. There was only one word worse than the P one.

"So does this mean you hate the word vagina too?"

"I swear, Bait, if you don't stop, I will let Johnson gag you."

"You wouldn't dare."

"Keep teasing me and you'll find out."

She went silent and stiff. He could practically scent her fear. Shit. So much for his plan to get her to trust him. He tried to ease her mind. "Relax. I wouldn't actually do that."

"How do I know you're not lying?"

He sighed. "You don't. But I can tell you right now that if I truly wanted to harm you or seduce you then you're hardly strong enough to stop me."

Once again, she went completely still. "You know, that really wasn't the most encouraging thing you could have said."

"No. It wasn't. And yet..." He nuzzled the back of her neck, his nose parting the hair until he could touch the skin of her nape. A shiver went through her. "For some reason, even though we keep clashing, you desire me."

"Do not."

"Don't forget, I'm a wolf. I can smell it."

"That's disturbing."

He couldn't help but laugh at the way she uttered it. "Only to those with a less than refined sense of smell. To those of us who live every moment with it, it's all part and parcel of how we perceive the world, and it influences our acts."

No denying scent, especially hers, certainly had an effect. Even though he'd yet to make up his mind on Layla, he couldn't stem his attraction to her. Not one bit.

Nuzzling her didn't help. Spooning her body to follow its every contour just made it worse. She ensorcelled him without doing a damned thing.

He wasn't alone in suffering from the attraction. "How do I make it stop?" she asked.

The idea that she couldn't help but want him made his longing even fiercer. He chuckled. "Easy. Don't desire me."

"I don't want to. But I can't seem to control it."

So grudgingly admitted. His wolf preened and wagged its tail, but Brody wanted to show his thanks in a more sensual fashion. He let his lips run over the skin of her neck. "Well, how about I help you with your problem? You don't have to worry about seducing me. I don't sleep with the enemy." Not entirely true. If the mission called for it, he would have sex. For Intel, of course.

He could almost hear his old sarge bark, *Boy, sometimes you've got to do ugly things. And sometimes you get to fuck pretty things. Just always remember, it's for the good of the mission.*

A sigh left her in a big rush of air. "I'm not the enemy. For you at any rate. You, however, are a problem."

If they weren't enemies, the possibilities expanded. Or not.

Brody needed to remind himself that, prisoner or not, she'd abetted in some crimes against the clan. "Even if we're both prisoners, it doesn't put us on the same side. You helped attack my town and the people I'm responsible for." In actuality, she'd done no worse than Gene. *And we managed to forgive him.* After punching and kicking him a few times to vent. Or, as Sarge would have called it, given him some tough love.

"I had to."

A disbelieving snort left him. "How did you have to launch wild wolves at people?"

"And bunnies. Don't forget the vicious bunnies."

His lips twitched. He would not think of the big-eared menaces that had swarmed the town. Good thing he liked rabbit stew. "This isn't funny."

"You're right, it's not. I'm sorry if I had to attack people you knew, but I did what I had to. I don't have many choices. And you might note that while my supposed side suffered numerous fatalities yours didn't as far as I know."

To that Brody snapped his mouth shut as he made that connection. "You mean, you purposely held back?"

"I'm not saying anything except apparently wild animals are no match for real shifters."

Brody clamped his lips as it suddenly occurred to him the girl was trying to avoid spilling secrets with a camera and microphone watching and listening to their every move.

But she had one fact wrong. "Someone did die. That first driver whose truck was hijacked back when everything started."

"Oh he wasn't killed by us. The bugger keeled over on his own. Bad ticker. Which is usually rare for your kind."

Rare, but not unheard of. While they did heal at a quicker rate than humans, they were still susceptible to imperfections and the signs of aging.

Given her loquacious mood, he decided to see what other information he could glean. Starting with her powers. "You control animals."

"And some insects, too."

"That's just weird."

"Weirder than howling at the moon and needing a flea bath?"

"I'll have you know, I get my flea and tick shot every spring before the season starts."

She couldn't completely mask her snort of amusement. "Good to know. I won't waste my time ordering my insects to bite you."

"So you can do small, what about big? How large of a beast can you control?"

"It's not the size that matters. It's my access to their mind and how strong their self-will is."

"Do you read it?"

Could she read his right now, which said they should put their mouths to better use than talking?

"No. I don't. And I really don't want to discuss it. If you don't mind, I'm going to sleep so I can enjoy my scintillating day of staring at the walls and electroshock therapy."

She pillowed her hands under head but didn't attempt to escape his grip.

Rest was a good plan. He needed a clear head. Who knew what tomorrow would bring? But he wasn't ready yet. He nudged at her to see if he could get her to resume talking. "I've noticed you're not afraid of speaking out. I'm surprised. Isn't some of this shit you're telling me secret?"

"Yes. But you don't have to worry. Master has no idea what we're saying."

"Um, in case you hadn't noticed, there's a camera watching us, and I would assume a microphone."

She giggled. "No microphone anymore. While I was reading this afternoon, I took care of it. It's the funniest thing. The spiders in this place keep gumming up the receiver."

Creepy or cool? He wasn't sure. "You can get them to web it? Why not do the camera, too, then?"

"Because the lens wipes off too easily, unlike the hole in the mic. Besides, I've found so long as he can see, he doesn't care about listening. And I don't have to spend a day sitting here sniffing the fumes from bug spray."

The more she revealed about her freaky powers, the less daunted he found himself, which he didn't understand. By all accounts, she was a dangerous weapon. In the wrong hands, like the current ones, she could really cause some havoc.

But telling a girl she was probably better off dead before she was forced to cause some kind of

Planet of the Apes rebellion with every fucking creature, and bug, on the planet probably wouldn't go over well. So he asked Layla the less offensive question. "How old are you?"

"Why do you care?"

"Just making conversation."

"More like profiling me I'll bet." How well she already knew him. "I'm twenty-three. And you?"

"Older."

"I see this conversation is going to be one-sided."

Her sarcastic snipes amused him. So he gave her a little. "I'm old enough to know that my snuggling with you under this blanket probably isn't a good idea."

"Why?"

"Because now I really have to kiss you."

He did.

Right now.

Before she could protest, he angled her head so his lips could find hers. The darkness didn't stop him. Neither did common sense. He could lie and say he did this as part of a plan to advance his cause, but really, he kissed her because he just couldn't handle being this close to her and not touching.

Her lips parted with a soft exhalation of surprise. He caught it and reveled in the warm breath, the essence of her mixing with his own. She tasted of the toothpaste she'd used to brush her teeth, still minty fresh, and yet, the spice at her core still managed to seep through.

It made him hunger.

He rolled her onto her back and partially covered her with his body, giving himself fuller access to her mouth. He plundered its soft recess, his tongue thrusting and sliding along hers while his hand skimmed the curves of her frame. To his groaning delight, she matched him for passion and ferocity.

As she clumsily fumbled, but learning quickly, their teeth clashed, and harsh pants mingled. No tempest ever raged so tumultuously.

Given her eager reception to his embrace, he gave in to another temptation. He allowed himself to cup the full breast he'd gotten hints of. It filled his hand. Spilled out of it. A perfect size.

Fuck, did he want to wrap his lips around the fat nipple he bet topped it? A grand idea.

He left the sweetness of her lips and grazed his way down the smooth column of her neck, noting the rapid flutter of her pulse. Encountering the collar, he was starkly reminded of their situation. But it didn't stop him.

Nothing could at this point, not with need thrumming through every inch of his body.

Still palming her heavy globe, he let his mouth skim the fabric hiding her breast until he hit the protrusion of her nipple. Then he latched on.

She cried out, her hands suddenly clasping his hair, tugging at it, encouraging him to suck some more. So he did, tweaking the tip with his teeth and then taking the covered bud into his mouth.

How he suddenly hated the gown that hid

her glorious assets from him.

His cock throbbed against Layla's lower belly, but not against skin.

Need to touch.

He let his hand travel down the length of her, skimming over curves he wished he could see, but at least could feel.

Reaching the edge of her gown, which had ridden up to mid thigh, he tugged at it, pulling higher, wanting to rid himself of this barrier.

He growled in annoyance and then wanted to slap himself.

Her whole body went rigid. She stopped breathing. Stopped squirming. And in the darkness he couldn't miss her horrified whisper. "What am I doing? We need to stop."

A true jerk would have ignored her feeble attempt to halt things. He could smell her desire, feel it in the heat that radiated from her skin and how her heart raced.

But, he wasn't an animal—most of the time. And especially not when it came to sex.

With Layla, though, abstaining from what they both needed—oh, how he needed—practically hurt. With gritted teeth, he turned away from her but didn't leave the bed. He still needed a place to rest and stay warm.

And she needed to get used to him.

Because it wasn't a lack of desire that made her turn away from him but rather the uncontrollable need, the loss of control. He could understand that because it freaked him out, too.

Since when did he let emotions overtake his

common sense? Since when did his selfish desires trump his safety?

Since I met my siren.

An apt name for her. Much like the creatures of legend, Bait enticed him but, in her case, with more than just her voice. She seduced him with her entire being.

Ack. So not ready. Commitment was something other men did. Men who liked to stay home and work mostly nine to five. Brody wanted more from life than a mundane existence.

And why was he even thinking of domestication—that bad, bad word?

I have one mission. Escape. Everything else is a distraction.

He rolled to his back beside her, listening to her breathe, counting the flutters of her heartbeat as it took its time slowing down. He could have stated with certainty when he knew sleep finally overtook her.

With the possibility of danger low, because there was no way he'd miss anyone approaching the cage, he allowed himself to close his eyes. He placed himself in a trance that rested but kept him partially aware.

Watch. Guard. His wolf would keep them safe.

Despite knowing his furry friend wouldn't let him down, slumber eluded him. He was fully aware when Layla turned and rolled against him in her sleep. She slung an arm and a leg over him, and he allowed himself to place his arms around her. He relaxed even further into his almost hypnotic state. And then…slept.

Chapter Six

Waking to find her face pressed against bare skin was new. Not unpleasant either. The hair on the chest she pillowed felt soft and springy, unlike the man. Flirty one minute, flinty the next.

Layla no longer knew what to think of Brody, other than he was dangerous.

Very, very dangerous.

Look at the previous evening for example. She'd allowed him to take liberties with her person. She'd not struggled once when he kissed her, or groped her, or done that really wicked thing with his lips and teeth on her breast.

On the contrary, why stop it when she wanted more? But she had put a halt to his advances. Needed to remember he was a stranger with an as-of-yet-unknown agenda.

To his credit, Brody immediately took heed, stopping his delightful torture, leaving her aching.

The yearning was almost a worse form of torture. It seemed to take forever before her body finally cooled enough to sleep. But, apparently, she'd managed to slumber because how else to explain why she found herself plastered against him, an arm and leg possessively draped, her face pressed against a pectoral, and his amused voice saying, "Morning, Bait."

"Is it? How can you tell in this blasted dark?" Did he have some special wolfy sense that let him track the rise and fall of the sun? No, that was vampires according to the books she'd read.

"It's easy to figure out. We're both awake, and I can hear footsteps upstairs and the toilet has been flushing."

Good clues. She'd appreciate them even better once she moved away from his distracting skin. Surely it wasn't normal to want to kiss it and lick it.

Her attempt to slide away saw him tightening the arms he'd strung around her.

"Where do you think you are going, Bait?"

Away from you. Before she did something embarrassing like ask him to finish what they began the previous eve. To hide her first thought, she went on the attack. "Why must you keep calling me Bait?"

"Because that's what you are. Bait dangled to snare a wolf."

"Not by choice."

"Says you."

"Yes, says me. So find another nickname."

"Fine then, *sweetheart.*" Funny how he could make a term of endearment sound so snarky.

Before she could comment on his maturity level, without warning, the lights flicked on and the speaker crackled to life. "How nice. My pet and her stud in bed together. I take it the deed was less onerous than expected."

Layla frowned at the camera and shook her head negatively, knowing the microphone wouldn't catch her words since she'd gotten her spidery friend to gum it the day before. "We didn't do anything." For some reason it seemed important to clarify this out loud. Maybe then it would make her more resistant.

It seemed master either read her lips or determined her intent. "Didn't do anything yet," corrected the robotic voice. "I have a feeling, though, it won't be long."

"He might be right," Brody whispered in her ear, sending a delicious shiver down her spine.

"No, he's not," she snapped, hoping she wasn't making a total liar of herself because, honestly, Brody upset her equilibrium on so many levels.

Wrestling free of the blankets, and managing to touch way more of Brody than she wanted, Layla got to her feet and stomped over to the sink to wash the sleep from her face. And, yes, pee as well, because nothing doused the libido like knowing a cute guy could hear her tinkling.

The blankets of the bed rustled as she stared at her toes while sitting on the cold plastic seat. At least her gown allowed her some measure of privacy. Not much. But she'd take it.

Done, she flushed and kept her gaze averted from him, not easy once she realized he was under the covers and, judging by the jeans on the floor, still naked.

"Are you coming back to bed?" he drawled as he patted the spot beside him. His eyes flashed as wickedly as the smile he shot her.

"No, thank you."

"Aw, why not? Bring one of those romance smut books with you. Maybe it will give you ideas." He waggled his brows.

"If this is your idea of seduction, forget it. That is not attractive." Actually, it was but, given his playful demeanor and the space between them, easy to rebuff.

"Just being friendly."

"You can keep your friendly. I don't trust you."

"The feeling's mutual, sweetheart, but we're stuck here together, so we need to learn to make the best of it."

Their conversation got interrupted as the door leading to the basement opened. Feet came tromping down the stairs, a full half-dozen men, which probably didn't bode well.

Field trip.

Naked or not, Brody bounded from the bed and took a stance in front of her. Did he think he could protect her? With what? His superbly tight butt? Maybe Johnson would rise to the occasion and smite the guards.

She bit her lip lest she giggle and averted her gaze, but it kept creeping back, fascinated not just by the perfection of the tight glutes but the tattoo emblazoned across one cheek.

What kind of man gets a pink bunny inked on his body?

"On your knees, hands behind your back," barked one of them.

"Make me," Brody dared, and she sighed.

Here we go.

The electrical zap in her collar hit her in a rush of pain, but she gritted her teeth and bore it. She knew the drill. She drew her hands together behind her and got on her knees, leaning forward. Some things weren't worth fighting.

Poor Brody, he never had a chance to comply. They buzzed his collar, and he hit the ground—*thud*—twitching. It seemed Mr. Tough Guy would need more practice before he could handle the shock. Only repeated sessions truly made a person resistant, and as soon as you were, they increased the jolt level.

Once shackled, she spared a look at Brody, only to gasp. The guards hadn't given him time to put some pants on before they zapped him. And it wasn't his bare butt facing her anymore. She caught a glimpse of corded thighs, springy dark hair at the vee and…*Oh my*. She looked away, not quick enough, though, to stop the blush.

The guards didn't seem to care about his nudity. They dragged his limp body, a man under each arm, from the cell. Layla moved on her own two feet. Again, she knew the routine. Given the number of guards and the precautions, she had an inkling of where they were going.

The master wanted to see them.

The men were not kind as they dragged her cellmate up the steps, banging him off every tread. Poor Brody's shins would bear bruises for as long as it took to heal them. She didn't dare say anything. If the master for one moment suspected she cared—*No, I don't*—for the wolf, he'd probably do something vile.

The living room, where her captor enjoyed holding court, hadn't changed much from previous meetings. Simply decorated and furnished, as simple as the rest of the house.

The walls were plaster, but old plaster, the kind slathered on and not so smooth, covered in peeling wallpaper, which in some spots revealed another layer of wallpaper beneath, faded orange and brown, splotchy flowers.

The wide-plank pine floors creaked as she walked on them, the varnish on their surface long gone, but the grime of feet sponged into the surface giving them a gritty texture.

The furnishings, given their ugliness, probably had never enjoyed better days. Orange, yellow, and green flowered cushions provided seating on one sofa, while brown corduroy, worn bare in some spots, covered matching club chairs.

They were familiar chairs. She'd sat in the left one many a time listening to the master's ranting and threats. To be contrary, she sat in the right-hand one, arms still manacled behind her back. The guards dumped Brody's still unconscious carcass in her usual seat, but he merited extra special treatment. A chain was brought forth, rattling as they locked it onto his handcuffs then attached it to a ring in the floor making sure Brody wouldn't get far if he attempted anything.

"Welcome, pet. You seem in high form this morn."

"If you mean plotting your demise, then

yes. Yes, I am doing great." She spoke with a smile, hoping it aggravated him. Hard to tell though, given she couldn't read the master's expression.

Perched dead center on the couch, he wore his customary black hood, not even the color of his eyes visible through the thick cloth. How did he breathe? Eat? Surely he took the covering off sometime?

Why does he hide? A question she'd often wondered but never had answered.

"Plot as much as you like, pet. You will never escape me." The machine-induced voice came from a spot around master's neck. She'd often wondered at the reason behind the modulated speech. Had he suffered some kind of injury that made it hard for him to speak?

"We'll see about that," she muttered.

"Your optimism after so many failures is fascinating. When will you admit defeat? When will you finally stop fighting and accept your fate, pet?"

"The day I stop fighting is the day I die."

"Death? How melodramatic, pet. Especially since I've now given you a cellmate. A lover to keep you company."

"Not happening."

"Think what you will, pet, although, it might help if he were less fragile. I see our new guest isn't faring well."

"A thousand volts will do that to a person," she replied dryly.

"And he'll get more if he doesn't do as he's told and bed you. Still, though, I expected a little more strength from him."

"Keep zapping him. I'm sure he'll eventually get used to it like I did. He might not prove the handy tool you hoped, though."

"What is that supposed to mean?"

She rolled her eyes. "You can't seriously think electrocuting him will aid your task."

"He's a Lycan. They heal quickly."

"He does, but…" Layla might lack experience in some respects, but it was amazing what one could learn in a book, even seemingly harmless romance ones. "Even if he does heal fast, what do you think all that electricity is doing to his, you know," she lowered her voice, "*stuff?*"

Not a wrinkle marred the surface of the fabric covering master's face, but Layla imagined he frowned.

"Does your concern over his ability to perform mean you're willing to obey?"

"No. I won't have sex with him." For at least a few hours until the lights turned out and he crawled in to bed with her. Then…who knew what would happen?

She really needed to execute a plan of escape before she found out.

"Defiance gains you nothing."

"But it irritates you. So, if you ask me, that's kind of a win."

"Insolent creature."

"Insolent. Disrespectful. Bitchy. Call me all the names you want, but it doesn't mean I'm going to play the part of whore."

The master moved fast. The sudden slap rocked her, but it was the snarled, "Don't touch her," that surprised her.

A certain wolf had woken, and he didn't seem pleased at all.

"It's awake." Even without a facial expression, one could hear the sneer in master's tone.

"Awake and irritable. Not a good combination. So I wouldn't push it if I were you."

"Threats? Yet you are in no position to make demands."

"That's what you think."

Layla could almost applaud his belligerence. But, while she knew from experience the master would never go so far as to permanently damage her, the same could not be said of Brody. As far as she knew, he was expendable when it came to the master's plans.

"I see we've yet to break your spirit. Excellent. I'd hate to think I chose wrong when selecting the man who will father babes on my pet."

"I won't do it."

"Then I'll find another," the master said, his robotic voice not giving any inflection, the monotone of it making it sound so much colder.

"There will be no others."

Layla almost shivered at the firm certainty in Brody's voice. A more fanciful girl would have romanticized it and called it possessive. But Layla was grounded in reality. More than likely, Brody would attempt to kill her first before letting master create an army of minions with her special brand of power.

"Again with the threats." The master shook his hooded head. "I will do whatever I like with my pet, and there is nothing you can do about it, wolf."

"Why are you doing this? Why keep her a prisoner? She's just a young girl. She doesn't deserve this kind of life."

"What's this? Are you concerned about the girl, dog? Then perhaps you should try harder to convince her to spread her legs. The sooner she is breeding, the faster she protects herself from the coming punishment I've got planned if she refuses to obey."

"She's not the only one unwilling."

"So I hear." The cloak figure leaned forward and placed himself close to Brody, close enough the wolf couldn't help but rumble. His body shook, restrained by the shackles that held him in place. "You will do as you're told, wolf, or else. I only have one use for you. Or at least a use for a certain part of your body. How much pride do you think you'll retain if I remove that crucial part your anatomy?"

Even Layla had to wince.

Poor Brody. The threat froze him. Only his nostrils flared as he breathed deeply in and out, a man fighting his wolf and his inclination to protect himself from a threat.

"No comeback, dog? No threats?"

"Just thinking of the best way to kill you," Brody bravely blustered.

The mechanical laugh from the master sent a shiver down her spine. "Think about it, but not too long, my pets. Already my patience wears thin and you don't want to see what happens when it snaps."

The interview was over. The master rose, his dark robe hiding his true shape and identity. With that awful glide, the master slithered from the room and left her alone for the moment with Brody.

"He's a pleasant dude," Brody remarked.

"A ray of sunshine," she muttered. "One you did your best to piss off."

"I can't stand pompous asses."

"Gee, I couldn't tell."

"Ah, come on, Bait, admit it, that was kind of fun."

"Don't call me bait. And no, it wasn't fun. You're new here. I don't think you grasp just how sadistic master can get."

"Oh, I can imagine. I've dealt with his sort before."

"So you're just an idiot with a death wish then."

"Nah, just an idiot with huge balls of steel. Wanna see?"

"No!"

He chuckled. "Let me know if you change your mind. Now that we've had the *talk* with the asshole in charge of this place, what's next on the agenda?"

"We wait until the guards come to take us back."

"Pretty trusting, leaving us here all by our lonesome."

"Not really. There's nowhere for us to go."

"Such pessimism."

"I call it realism." Also known as experience. She had numerous failed escapes from this room to attest to the futility.

But Brody was a man. Stubbornness was in his genes. "Mind telling me where the front door is?"

"Why do you need to know?" she asked.

"You'll see."

She glanced at him to find him smiling. "You find our situation amusing?"

"More like interesting."

"How do you figure that?"

"For one thing, we're out of the cage."

"Yet handcuffed and you're chained to a floor bolt. I fail to see the improvement."

"Again with the Negative Nelly attitude. You'll never succeed in escaping if you don't try. Now, I'm asking again, before Jackass and his friends show up, where's the front door?"

It wouldn't hurt to tell him. "Out in the hall, turn left, through the door into the screened porch and then left again. But I don't know what you think you can do with that information."

"Watch a master escape artist at work, sweetheart." He winked as he shifted his shoulders and drew his legs up in a tuck that allowed him to bring his cuffed hands forward. Brody then unlinked his chains—one for each manacled wrist—from the eyebolt in the floor.

She sighed. So he'd figured out the weakness in chains, not something she'd played with yet, as she hadn't wanted to attempt escape fifty-seven until she thought of a way to avoid the dilemma she'd run into with escape forty-nine.

Namely—

Too late to warn Brody as he was dashing through the door. She sat there and counted. One. Two. Three.

Thud.

A moment later, a pair of guards passed by the archway to the living room where she sat, dragging Brody's limp carcass down the hall. Another pair arrived shortly after to fetch her.

But it seemed they weren't returning to their cell quite yet.

They both got dumped in the bathroom with its large shower stall, lined in cracked pink and black tile, and its clawed tub. Once again familiar with this part of the routine, she presented her back to the guards so they could remove the cuffs she still wore.

The master had learned early on that a slippery shower and no hands for balance didn't make a good combination. Her subsequent concussion and stitches made him revise her bathing ritual.

This was one place she never tried to escape from. For one thing, the window was nailed shut and too small. Secondly, the guards were right outside the door with the trigger for her collar. Since she appreciated the chance to get clean, especially given how randomly it happened, she behaved.

And she usually bathed alone.

She eyed Brody's limp body on the floor
and wondered if she had time to shower quickly
before he awoke.

Nope.

A groan rocked him first. He shook his
head and slurred. "What the fuck happened?"

"You didn't listen."

"Listen to what?"

"Sometime after escape forty-eight, they put
a collar trigger on all the doors exiting the house."

"And you couldn't tell me this before I ran
right into it?"

She shrugged. "I told you it was impossible,
and you never gave me a chance to explain why.
You just bolted out of there. If you ask me, I think
you deserved it."

"Deserved getting zapped like a mosquito?"

"Yes, because you left me behind. So much
for taking me with you when you left." A little
miffed that he'd bolted without looking back?
Damned straight.

"I was going to come back for you."

"Sure you were." She didn't bother to mask
her sarcasm. Reaching out, she spun the levers for
the water. She knew from experience she wouldn't
get much time to cleanse herself.

"Don't you try and guilt me, sweetheart.
What other nasty surprises did you neglect to tell
me about?"

"I didn't neglect. I just didn't bother. I told
you escape hadn't worked." Turning her back on
him, she pretended he wasn't there as she shed her
gown and stepped into the tepid water shooting in

bursts from the showerhead.

"Not for you maybe, but I…" His voice tapered as he finally noted her actions. "What are you doing?"

Keeping her back to him, she focused on the bar of soap in her hands, lathering it soundly and rinsing it before daring to lay it on her skin. Who knew what grubby hands touched it before?

"I'm showering."

"Now?"

"Yup. I don't often get a chance so excuse me if I jump on it."

"Haven't you ever watched a horror movie?"

"What's that got to do with me showering?"

"Judging by that reply, I'm going to guess the answer is no."

"No. I haven't." She'd missed out on a lot of things other people took for granted. If it wasn't in a book, or part of the master's plan, then chances were she'd never experienced it.

"Well, in horror movies, only the stupid girl showers when in the psycho's house. Usually only minutes before she dies. Horribly. Screaming."

Layla soaked her hair before replying. "But at least she's clean."

"You are seriously demented."

"A product of my environment. If you don't like it, leave. Oh wait. You can't." She still wore her smirk when he spun her around and glared at her.

"This isn't amusing."

Her lips stretched wider. "Depends on your perspective. From where I'm standing, it's hilarious, Thud."

"Thud?" His brow crinkled.

"I think that should be your new nickname because that's the sound you make every time they juice your collar and you hit the floor."

"I do not."

"Sure you don't…Thud." She snickered. How could she help it when he tried to hold his glare, which really wasn't all that effective with his mouth hanging open in slack-jawed amazement. "Do you mind if I finish showering? There's probably not much time left." She turned her back and resumed soaping, only to squeak as a distinctly naked body pressed in against her from behind.

"What are you doing?" she demanded, unable to turn as he snaked an arm around her middle and kept her firmly in place.

"As you keep pointing out, we won't get much time to shower. I think it's best if we make the most of the time we have by sharing."

"This isn't sharing. This is you hogging my water. How am I supposed to wash myself like this?"

"Let me." Masculine fingers plucked the soap and lathered it. One-handed, he then stroked the suds down her arms.

"So tell me, Layla. What other surprises have you neglected to share?"

Perhaps if she concentrated on past failures she could ignore the present, namely the erotic sensation his hand caused as it rubbed soap against her skin. His bare skin against her. His body pressed—

She swallowed hard. "You met the zap trigger at the front door. There's one at the back, too. But that door's also locked, deadbolted with a key on the inside, so not a feasible exit."

"And he's got the windows nailed shut."

"Nailed and, in some cases, plywood covering them."

"Have you ever made it outside?"

She nodded, her breath quickening as his hand stroked soapy circles on her belly. It was so hard to think with him touching her like this. "Yeah. I've made it outside a few times before he put the collar trigger on the doors. If you get past the screen porch, then you've got to watch out for a couple of huskies he keeps," she confessed in a rush. His languorous rubs over her skin, even something as innocuous as her belly, had the oddest effect. She tried to ignore the heated liquid pooling between her thighs, the warmth of it much more scorching than this shower.

"Dogs, eh? I can handle those."

"But they're just a distraction from the men with the tranquilizer guns who guard the perimeter of the yard." She'd learned about those in escape fifty-three. According to the master, they were placed there after her botched escape number forty-five.

Each time she failed, the master plugged the weakness she'd exploited.

Brody brushed a hand over her breasts, teasing the taut buds and making her breath catch.

"Tell me more," he practically purred in her ear.

The whisper of his breath weakened her knees. "We're about fifteen miles from the nearest small town."

"Only fifteen?"

"Yes, and it's not much of a place. Just a few houses, one general store."

"Anything closer?"

"There is a cabin, about eight miles west. It means diverting from a straight beeline to town, but it's good for supplies." Escape number thirty-nine. She'd never returned. Food and clothes didn't get her far on foot.

"More. I *need*"—his hand glided down the slope of her body and he tickled the top of her pubes—"more. What about phones? Do the guards carry any?"

She swallowed and closed her eyes. She didn't want to react to his touch. Didn't want to feel anything for him. Didn't want to sleep with him. Damn him for making this so hard.

"The cellphones they have are programmed to call only one number, and it's not the police."

Nothing like dialing 911 and having the master's robotic voice greet her with a chiding, "Bad, pet."

As Brody cupped her sex, a shudder rocked her body. His lips practically caressed her earlobe as he said, "I want more, sweetheart. Give it to me. Give it all."

As his finger stroked, seesawing back and forth against her flesh, she couldn't help but lean her head back. "There's a sniper on the roof. He's a pretty good shot."

"More."

Yes, more. "There's a ravine to the northeast. It drops into a deep river with a pretty fast current."

She found that one by accident during escape thirty-eight.

The finger stroking her concentrated on one stimulating spot, and she couldn't help but moan and rock her hips.

"That's it, sweetheart. Just a little bit more."

"He…He…" The delightful torture kept wiping the words from her tongue.

He stopped rubbing. She could have cried.

"He what, Layla?"

"He has a few trucks in the garage, and I think the guards also have some dirt bikes." Which she didn't know how to drive so they were useless to her.

Apparently that information pleased Brody because his finger resumed its torturous play, rubbing against her pleasure button, his throbbing shaft pressing against her backside. His lips tugged and sucked at her ear lobe. But when his second hand left her waist and took up a new position, the fingers sliding into her slick heat…

An orgasm rocked her. It had to be an orgasm because she'd never had such absolute bliss shoot through her body. Her whole body tensed and flexed, pulsed in time with her shuddering waves of pleasure, leaving her whimpering and weak.

Yet not alone because Brody was there to hold her.

His arms wrapped around her wet frame, his lips brushing her temple as he murmured soft words to her. She relaxed against him because, for some reason, she just knew he wouldn't let her fall.

For a moment she dared to imagine him never letting her go. If only.

Chapter Seven

The problem with playing dirty for answers was it left Brody even worse off than before.

Can blue balls explode?

He'd probably soon find out if he didn't get relief soon.

And why wasn't he taking care of his rigid problem? After all, here Brody was, holding a limp Layla, who'd just come on his hand, her sex squeezing his fingers so deliciously. She was ripe for fucking. Willing and so responsive. A less noble man might have taken the moment to give her something a little thicker to grip.

But Brody had two problems with that.

One. While pleasuring her for Intel barely squeaked under his moral radar, fucking her to relieve himself crossed a line. Especially since he'd come to the conclusion she truly was an innocent in this affair, which meant he couldn't treat her like an enemy. In other words, no seduction. But not being the enemy didn't mean she trusted him, hence his less-than-honorable methods in getting her to talk—and come.

Cupping her still pulsing mound, Brody couldn't bring himself to move away. Nor did she seem in a hurry. She moaned and even wiggled her hips. An invitation to proceed, which might have canceled out problem number one if not for problem number two.

Their unexpected interruption.

"Time's up," barked Caveman as he slammed the bathroom door open.

A protective instinct—tinged with a hint of jealousy—saw Brody tucking Layla behind him as he turned to face the guard who stood belligerently in the doorway.

"Do you mind?" Brody said. "The lady and I aren't done."

"But I says you are," drawled the fat-faced idiot.

"Leave now before you force me to hurt you."

"Bring it, dog boy."

Brody sighed. "You bloody seal shifters and your pea-sized brains. I should have known you wouldn't listen."

His fist shot out and connected with a solid thwack on the asshat's temple. Satisfying, but it didn't go unpunished. Here came the getting familiar sizzle. Brody relaxed his muscles and let the current take over. He'd master it this time. He'd—

Thud.

He hit the floor and jiggled, more aware than he let on, peeking at the situation through slitted eyes, which in turn gave him an interesting view of Layla's private parts.

Mmm tasty.

Not now. But maybe later if he needed to, he'd indulge in a snack, for the mission of course.

Layla apparently wasn't into exhibitionism, as she quickly whipped a towel from a bar and wrapped it around her body. Then she straddled him, hands on her hips. "Stop that right now."

"You're not the one giving orders," Jackass replied, his thumb holding down the button on a remote.

"But I am the one expected to bed him, and he's useless to me if you turn him in to a vegetable."

"I'll bed you if you're so desperate for a man." Caveman had recovered from the punch to his face, as crude as ever. He grabbed his crotch lewdly, and Brody really had to restrain himself from lunging and removing the guy's dick permanently.

Make rude advances on his woman, would he? Brody would show him.

We'll kill him.

His wolf totally thought it was a fine plan, but rashness never paid off. Brody stayed his initial murderous impulse. The situation wasn't ripe yet for attack or escape. He needed to exercise patience.

His wolf pouted.

Hell, Brody pouted. He really wanted to hit Caveman again.

A moue of distaste twisted Layla's next words. "Why do men think that's attractive? I mean, really, grabbing your crotch? How is that sexy? What would you think if I grabbed myself?"

Oh, please do.

"I can grab it for you," said Caveman with a leer.

"You aren't touching me. Ever. I despise you. I hate you so much I wouldn't spit on you if you were on fire, and I most certainly would never have sex with you."

"I never said you had to be willing."

Pretending comatose or not, Brody almost didn't let that threat fly. But Layla was proving herself capable when it came to sticking up for herself.

"I dare you to try. Come on. Let's see how brave you are because you can't tell me no one told you what happened to the last guy who thought he could force me. Who knew testicles were such a delicacy for the rats?"

Ouch. Caveman wasn't the only guy who winced. Brody barely restrained himself from cupping his own exposed sac.

Jackass cuffed the Neanderthal in the back of the head. "Leave the girl alone. She's not the only one who'll have your fucking balls if you lay a single finger on her."

"Says the guy still pouring the juice into dickwad over here. The master warned us to keep the wolf alive. And in good shape. He won't be too happy if he finds out you've ruined his plans."

The current faded, yet Brody still feigned unconsciousness. It didn't prevent the cuffs from getting placed around his wrists, or Layla's, but at least he managed glimpses of their current location. He noted doorways and did his best to sift scents, separating fresh from old so he could try and estimate numbers.

He bit back some winces as they dragged him none too nicely down the wooden steps, scraping his shins. They'd pay for that when he escaped.

And he would escape.

A plan was forming. A plan he'd attempt real soon.

Back in their cage—home sweet home—the guards zapped them into compliance, unshackled them, and left.

Brody counted to three thousand so that anyone watching wouldn't guess their little zap trick wasn't working anymore before rolling on to his back and grinning at her. "So, when does your ravishing of my male parts begin?"

Chapter Eight

"Why you faker!" Why Layla was shocked at his possum play, she couldn't have said. She'd thought it odd a big, strong guy like him succumbed so thoroughly to the zapping collars. She just assumed it affected shifters differently or that they had him on a higher voltage.

"Fake? Who me?" Brody attempted an innocent look.

As if it worked. She doubted he'd managed wide eyed innocence in years, if not decades.

"You can cut the puppy eyes. It won't work."

"What if I jutted my lower lip and batted my lashes?"

She snickered. "That's just wrong."

He grinned. "Fine. So I played possum."

Wet strands of hair swung as Layla shook her head. "They're going to catch on. Or had you forgotten the camera in here?"

"I didn't forget, but I did notice on the way in that the lens got webbed while we showered."

He'd noticed? She'd actually given the mental order to her eight-legged minion before they left the cell. Given master's interest in her and

Brody, she thought it best if he not have the ability to spy at all because, despite herself, she was interested in the wolf, and she knew their conversations, while often argumentative in nature, were stimulating. Too stimulating.

"They can still see a bit."

"Which is why I faked being passed out even after they dumped me in here."

"You're playing a dangerous game."

"The best kind, sweetheart. But don't worry. We'll be long gone before those idiots figure it out."

"Oh really? And exactly how do you plan to manage that?"

"Are you ready to be impressed with my excellent strategy?"

"No, more like looking forward to poking holes in it."

He clutched his chest. "You wound me. But it's okay. I'll live. Here's the plan. We leave tomorrow morning when they bring breakfast. I was going to tell you to gum the camera with your little spider buddy overnight, but you've already taken care of that. Although it wouldn't hurt to maybe add an extra layer. When the guards come in the morning and give me my morning jolt of electricity, I'll fake my little jiggle. Then, when they open the cage, I'll rush them and knock them out."

"Wouldn't it be more prudent to kill them so they don't come after us?"

A grin stretched his lips. "A lady after my own heart. Yes, it would be more prudent, but I thought if I told you that part of the plan you'd go all girly on me. I was sparing your delicate sensibilities."

Ah, how sweet. He'd used the word delicate in reference to her. It made her next words all the more ironic. "They'd hurt or kill me in an instant if ordered. So I say, twist their necks or rip out their hearts, or whatever it is you Lycans do."

"Thank you, I think."

"Don't thank me yet because, even if you kill them, I don't see how you plan to escape." She played Devil's advocate. "Let's say you make it out of this cage and then upstairs. You still can't get out. The doorways will still trigger your collar. And even if they didn't, have you forgotten the sniper on the roof and the dogs?" She itemized each of the roadblocks, and it didn't budge his smile one bit.

"Don't worry, sweetheart. I've got a plan." Cocky confidence oozed from him.

"Why am I not reassured?" she muttered.

"Trust me."

"Sorry, but I don't trust anyone but myself."

"Fair enough. But I'm telling you this plan will work. It's not ideal. I mean, I would have preferred we leave at night, under the cover of darkness, but since I can't pick the lock—"

"You want out of the cage at night? I can help with that."

Interrupted, he ogled her a moment. "What do you mean you can help?"

"I can take care of the lock on the cage door."

It took him a moment of staring at her before he replied. "You mean you've had a way out all this time and never said a word?"

She lifted her shoulders. "I was saving it because, like I told you, once I play that card, steps will be taken to prevent it on my next escape." And yet, here she was telling Brody about it. Was she stupid? Or just curious to see if perhaps having someone else in charge of the escape for once would make a difference?

"So do you have a key stashed around here or something?"

"Let's just say there's no lock that my little bug friends can't infiltrate and disable."

"That's brilliant."

The amazement in his tone warmed her more than it should have. "Yeah, well, it's also not something I like to advertise. Like I said, I was saving it for when I had a proper escape plan in place."

"Which we now do."

"Says you."

"Knows me. Trust me."

Trust? Such a simple request, and yet, Layla couldn't help the doubt. No one she'd trusted in the past ever came through for her. But how she wanted to believe.

More questioning wouldn't get him to reveal the rest of his plan. He kept replying with, "Don't worry. I've got it covered."

Having never had a partner for escape before, she gave him the benefit of the doubt. Except for one thing. "You keep saying you're bringing me with you, but you seem to have forgotten something. A certain tracking device in my body."

"I hadn't forgotten. I just hadn't gotten to that part of the plan yet. As soon as the lights go out, I'll remove it."

"Excuse me? One, where is it, and two, how the hell do you plan to do it? With your teeth?" The idea of him gnawing on her flesh shouldn't have made her shiver in pleasure.

"I spotted it in the shower and felt it when we were making out."

Making out. What a trite description of the inferno he'd caused to rage in her body.

"So you found it. That still doesn't tell me how you're going to remove it."

"Yeah, that part you probably won't like."

She narrowed her gaze. "Tell me."

"Do I have to?" He tried giving her puppy dog eyes again.

She glared.

He held up his hands in surrender. "No need to give me a death stare. In order to extract it, I'm going to have to shift my hands—which isn't easy I'll have you know. Only strong shifters in tune with their other half can do it."

"Give the wolf a bone. Would you like me to applaud your skill?"

"No respect," he mumbled.

She cocked her head and cupped a hand to her ear. "Do you hear that?"

"What?"

"It's the world's tiniest violin playing a tune

for you. Get over yourself. Once you shift your hands, then what?" Although she feared she already knew the answer.

"My claws are sharp enough to slice through your skin. One little gash and I'll pop the tracker out."

A wince twisted her lips. "Sounds like it will hurt."

"Yeah. It probably will." He didn't sugarcoat it.

"Won't that make me bleed?"

"Again, yes, which is why we have to wait for darkness. Then no one can see me doing it, and we can wash out the wound and bind it with the sheets."

She didn't like this part of his plot, but she knew Brody had to do it if escape fifty-seven was to have even a glimmer of hope.

"This plan better work," she grumbled.

"It will."

And if not, there was always attempt fifty-eight.

The rest of the day passed with agonizing slowness. She tried to read while he napped, but she kept finding her gaze straying to him. At least he'd put pants on. But it didn't erase the memory of what she'd seen and felt.

How she wanted to pretend he didn't appeal. That he didn't arouse. But everything about him fascinated her. Even their arguments.

Supper time came with its usual zap, which rendered her obedient—she couldn't control anybody, not even a tiny fly when the current rocked her. Brody hit the floor with his usual thud.

She found it hard to eat as excitement, tinged with dread, tightened her tummy into a ball.

As her internal clock began insisting lights out approached, she prepared for bed, just managing to hit the sheets before darkness hit with its usual suddenness.

For a moment, silence reigned, and she almost held her breath, which was silly. No one could hear her right now except for Brody. Brody, who was somewhere in the dark, possibly already transforming his hands into primitive surgical instruments.

What if he screws up, and I bleed to death?
What if the tracker is too deep?
This is going to hurt.

"Ready, sweetheart?"

Not really, but she'd still try. There was no point in trying to escape while that thing was inside her.

She lay on her stomach and felt Brody kneel by her side. His hand came to rest on the middle of her back. Even with her gown between them, she could feel the difference in the shape and texture.

"You need to pull this up."

As she tugged her gown up to her shoulders, only blushing slightly in the darkness as she bared her body, she heard the sound of material ripping.

"Are you lying down again?" he asked.

"Yes."

"I'm doing this by feel, which is not the best-case scenario."

"You can do this, right?" She sought reassurance.

"I think so."

She stiffened.

He chuckled. "Relax. This will work. So long as you don't flinch."

"Just do it," she muttered through clenched teeth.

The tip of a nail dragged across her upper left shoulder blade. She held her breath at the pressure of the slice and sharp pain as he punctured skin.

Warm liquid rolled down her side.

She squeaked before she buried her face in the pillow, biting down on the spongy material. His claw probed in the opening, really not a pleasant sensation.

Just when she wanted to scream, "Stop!" he withdrew.

"Got it."

Breathing through the pain, it took her a moment to reply. "You did?" Yeah, she sounded surprised. She'd not actually expected it to work.

"Of course. I'm going to leave it in your bed instead of crushing it. It might buy us some time."

Done playing canine doctor on her back, Brody used the strips of cloth he'd ripped to bind her wound, which now only emitted a dull throb.

As he worked, Layla kept her mind occupied, sending her multi-legged minion to work, gumming the camera lens further to buy them extra time in the morning in case no one noted their nocturnal escape. She also got her spider to click the tumblers to the locking mechanism on the cage.

Those things accomplished, they then sat and waited. Lights out for them didn't mean the household above them went to bed. Footsteps wandered. Water rattled the pipes. Only when the sounds of activity died down did Brody finally deem it safe enough—what a misnomer—for them to venture out of the silver prison.

Despite her misgivings, Layla couldn't help the glimmer of hope that insisted this escape would succeed.

Imagine what it would be like to finally be free.

She couldn't. But she sure wanted to see what it felt like.

Brody didn't need to place his fingers on her lips for her to know quiet was necessary. As he led her through the pitch-black basement, his strong fingers laced through hers, she had to trust he wouldn't walk her into a wall.

She made it to the stairs without bashing her face. With one hand braced against the stone blocks to guide her, she let her bare feet do the rest, stepping slowly on to each stair tread as they made their way to the top, where a tiny sliver of light outlined the door.

"Stay." He whispered the word, and she halted a few steps below him.

She knew what lay beyond the door. A kitchen. Not a very pretty one with grimy white cabinets, most missing their doors , a pitted wooden countertop, and a rickety round table with a few chairs, usually manned by a pair of guys playing cards or eating.

Leaning against the stone wall, she strained to hear if anyone awaited them on the other side of the door.

Not a sound. Not even the snore of a sleeping guard. Which made the creak of the hinge as Brody swung open the door super loud. But it wasn't as loud as the uttered, "What the f—"

Crack. Thump.

At Brody's beckoning hand, Layla climbed the rest of the steps and stepped into the room.

A body lay on the floor, Stickboy staring sightlessly.

One down.

Judging by the continued silence, no one suspected anything was amiss.

Brody winked at her as he again placed his finger on his lips in a shushing gesture. On bare feet, he eased to the doorway leading out to the rest of the house. He peeked and sniffed.

But at least he didn't mark the wall to show he'd been there.

She stuffed a fist in her mouth, lest she let out a giggle.

While he checked the hall, she perused the door in the kitchen that led outside. The shiny new deadbolt was drawn and required a key to unlock. A precaution installed since one of her escapes.

She called her little spider minion to take care of it, but lost her train of thought when Brody grasped her by the arm and tugged her in the opposite direction.

What was he doing? Where was he going? The door to escape was behind them.

He must have seen the confusion because he took a moment to pause and only a hairsbreadth from her ear whispered, "No doors because of the shock collars."

Good reason, but still no doors? That left windows that were painted or nailed shut. No way would he escape without making a racket.

It looked as if she'd have to start planning escape fifty-eight after all. Despite her conviction they would fail, she allowed him to lead her on tiptoe down the hall. He ignored the door to the bathroom, the window in there too small for either of them. He ignored the silent dining room and the living room.

Where did he stop? In front of the one closed door in the place. The one that held a pair of bunk beds for guards to sleep in. She'd seen the space before on one of her many parades past it to visit with the master.

Given the time of night, there was no way the room wouldn't hold any occupants. It didn't stop the crazy wolf.

He eased the door open, letting loose the sounds of several men sleeping, their snores and wheezing breaths giving their presence away.

She didn't enter with Brody, especially not once she saw the glint of the knife in his hand, a knife he'd either pilfered from the kitchen or from the body he'd left behind.

It took him mere moments to do his thing. He then beckoned her into the space. Even her less-than-refined nose recognized the coppery stink of blood.

She clamped her lips and wouldn't allow either horror at his actions or pity to affect her. These men were vile. Criminals and thugs. They'd gotten only what they deserved.

Brody closed the door behind her and went to the window, which gaped a few inches, the cool evening air wafting in. It seemed he'd found the one window in the house that still worked.

Fresh air, how she loved it. It was one of the highlights when the master brought her out to perform his evil bidding.

Brody leaned in close to impart some instructions. "When we get outside," not *if*, "you take care of the dogs you said he keeps around while I take care of the sentries."

She nodded.

Grasping the wooden sash, Brody heaved. The wood, warped by weather and time, wouldn't budge. He pushed again, and this time the window shot up, the noise loud in the silent night.

A voice from outside called out. "What the fuck was that?"

To her surprise, Brody answered, albeit sporting an accent she'd only ever heard her captors use. "Fucking pinhead farted in here again. I swear I'm going to fucking kill him, eh."

Apparently, his answer satisfied because a masculine laugh erupted from outside. "That's what happens when you eat beans for lunch and dinner."

Brody crouched by the window, watching

the darkness outside. Meanwhile, Layla couldn't help the creeping horror factor of being in a room with several bodies. Dead bodies. Bodies she could touch if she reached out a hand.

And what if they reached out first?

Her breathing quickened, and Brody noted it.

"Calm yourself, sweetheart. We'll be out of here in a minute. You ready to make some puppies roll over and have their bellies scratched?"

That was right. She had a task. *Take care of the master's dogs.*

She nodded her head, despite the darkness, guessing from her experience with wolves that he'd discern it. They could see much better than her in the absence of light.

"Let's go then."

Brody eased through the rectangular casement first and dropped to the ground. Inching to the window, she peeked out and could faintly make out his hands held out to catch her.

As if she needed help climbing. She'd clambered out of tighter, higher spots. But she didn't argue the masculine hands that gripped her around the waist and brought her to the ground.

He didn't linger. Off he padded to do whatever came next in his plan, which, she had to admit, was doing pretty good so far.

But I've gotten farther than this before and still managed to fail.

This time, though, she wasn't alone. Maybe this time could be different.

Out in the open, it wasn't hard for her to

cast her senses and find the minds of the dogs, sleeping in a heap on the porch. They already knew her mental touch and thus didn't fight it as she soothed their impulse to bark at the wolf they scented encroaching on their territory. She eased their mouth-watering hunger as the scent of blood enticed.

Sleep. It's all but a dream. No one to see here. No reason to bark.

A pity she couldn't hypnotize herself. She squeaked when a furry nose nudged her hand. Brody had shifted into his wolf.

A low growl emanated from the fluffy pile of dogs, the primal instinct to protect themselves from an animal higher on the food chain almost wrenching her grip on them. She soothed the huskies' fear.

The wolf wandered off, blending into the deep shadows. She wondered where Brody went and what he planned to do.

It was an odd quirk of her power that while she could virtually *see* animals and some insects, humans and shifters were blind to her unless she saw them through the eyes of the animals she controlled or her own, plain old human, eyesight.

She bit back a scream as Brody nosed her again, this time urging her to move away from the house, where there was still no sign of alarm.

It seemed almost too easy. Then again, given Brody's penchant for not leaving anyone alive to announce their escape, perhaps not. Still, unease plagued her even as her fingers tangled in the thick fur surrounding his neck and clasped the collar he still wore. He guided her around the house to the garage.

Surely he wasn't thinking of stealing a truck? The noise alone would announce far and wide their escape.

She stumbled when he halted. The fur on his back bristled and brushed her hand. What did he hear? Straining to hear, she had to admit defeat as not a sound broke the silence.

He shook her free and padded away in the darkness, leaving her alone to shiver and hug herself.

What am I doing? I should be running. Without Brody?

Why not? Sure, he'd gotten them this far— *with my help*—but ultimately, he had a different objective than her. As far as she knew, he planned to bring her back to Kodiak Point, where perhaps she'd end up a prisoner again.

Never.

I have a better idea. While he's distracted, I should strike out on my own.

Would he waste time tracking her down? Or would he try and put as much distance as he could between himself and the master?

Brody said to trust him.

But if she did and he lied?

Before she could talk herself out of it, her feet were moving. She cast her senses forth and settled on some nocturnal creatures winging overhead to serve as her warning eyes.

Bats, while blind, possessed incredible radar senses when it came to noting other hot-blooded creatures. With them flying ahead of her, she had them seek out possible traps, also known as people with guns.

But it seemed Brody was thorough. She almost stumbled over one dead body on her flight, then nothing. Nothing but branches and darkness and a pounding heart.

No warning cries came from behind her.

Nothing out of place tingled the senses of the bats she controlled.

It was just her, alone in the forest, fleeing. Without a tracking device!

Oh my god. I'm escaping. It's happening. It's—

A sharp crack broke the silence. One gunshot. Then two. Then some yells.

It seemed Brody had gotten noticed.

Damn it.

She quickened her pace, ignoring the stitch in her side as she ran, her bare feet protesting the abuse of rocks and twigs against her soles. Bruises and scratches would heal. She needed to keep moving. Needed to get as far as she could. *I also need to hide my trail.* For that, she needed water. Even a creek would do to mask her scent.

And quick, because that was the sound of a dirt bike. Make that dirt bikes coming after her.

I can't let them catch me.

She sent out a mental mission. There wasn't much around here, the master having exhausted most of the wildlife in the area. But she did have her aerial minions who took off, ironically, like bats out of hell.

Chapter Nine

The garage Brody entered, which was in better shape than the house, had a few more men in it than expected. They were also more alert. The squeak of the door as Brody pawed it open didn't go unnoticed, but at least the guy who got off a shot had shitty aim. The bullet went whizzing by his ear, as opposed to causing some difficulties by hitting something vital.

One missed bullet. He wasn't out of the woods yet. It would only take one lucky shot to put a wolf down.

In he charged, teeth bared, hackles bristling, and ready to cause some damage. He dashed at the gunman, who popped up from the bed of his pickup truck with a loaded shotgun.

Boom!

A few stray pellets stung his hide—*and wrecked my beautiful fur!*—but the majority missed, and he leapt to the bed of the truck. One good chomp was all it took to stop a guy he'd never seen before from firing ever again.

The next dude proved a little harder to deal with, given he slept in the loft above. Wolves and ladders didn't exactly go well together. He'd have to climb because the little prick wasn't coming down.

With no choice, Brody ducked behind a wheel well and shifted to his human shape. It almost cost him as a missile grazed the tip of his shoulder. It would heal. The hole he put in the shooter's forehead once he snagged his dead buddy's gun? Not so much.

Two down, not bad, except for the fact a third, a gutless seal, ran off screaming for help. Coward.

Time to get his ass moving before Brody discovered just how many men really were roaming around. He'd already taken out quite a few, but according to his nose, there were plenty more moving in and out of the area. Troublemakers and clan outcasts, who banded under the hooded one in charge, determined to cause chaos.

I need to tell Reid what I know. And get Layla away before she was forced to do more damage to Kodiak Point.

On foot, they'd never make it far enough. Speed was of essence. He quickly analyzed his options, aware of the distant shouts and slams of doors. He had only moments before he'd have company.

The pickup truck was out of commission with the flat tire the idiot in the loft gave it. That left an SUV and a battered four-door sedan, plus a pair of dirt bikes. Given he preferred to remain off the main roads, he shot the tires on the four-wheeled vehicles, rendering them useless for the moment.

They would have provided a comfortable ride, his wolf chided.

Screw comfort. Brody needed cross-country versatility, the kind he could get with two wheels.

His wolf snorted at his justification.

Okay, you caught me, he told his furry friend. It wasn't just about practicality. Brody just loved dirt biking.

Soaring off a hillock, hitting with a hard thump, the excitement of dipping and weaving? Good times. Times that resulted in more than a few scrapes, bruises, and broken bones. He'd come home after those incidents to hear his mother shake her head and tsk. "Boys and their toys."

Less toy in this situation than tool—fun tool that used gas and went *Vroom.* His man card swelled in pride.

Given the unknown terrain, two rugged wheels with a forgiving suspension would totally work. And it also meant Layla would have to hold on tight.

As he strode, naked as the day of his birth, he wished he had time to grab some clothes. Riding bare-assed on a motor bike wouldn't prove comfortable. Vinyl style seats rubbed. Ow. And he'd rather not recall the reason he knew this, although it had proved a valuable lesson. He'd never touched Uncle Jay's moonshine again. Hell no, not when his ass ached every time he thought of it.

Brody grabbed the first dirt bike and prayed it had gas. It felt kind of light, but the one behind it sloshed nicely. It would have to do because he was out of time. He needed to get Layla out of here because the remaining enemy in the house had hit the outside.

Speaking of his lady bait, what were the chances Layla still waited for him? He knew he took a chance of her slipping away while he dealt with transportation, but a part of him hoped she wouldn't. That she would trust him, although he couldn't have said why this was important.

What if she ran?

His wolf practically danced in excitement. *Chase.*

Run if you want, Bait. Hide. We do so love to seek.

Awoo.

Of course, chasing was only fun when he was the one on the hunt. In this case, he still needed to shake some miscreants off his tail.

Brody had no sooner wheeled the bike clear of the garage when the first bullet hit the ground to his left.

"Missed," he hollered, the taunt making him grin. Nothing like pissing off the enemy and getting them to fire wildly. He also liked to tempt fate—and dance with death.

Adrenaline coursed through his veins and gave him the illusion of invincibility. Knowing it was a false euphoria didn't stop him from adding fuel to the taunt by yelling, "Come and get me, you gutless cowards." Another bullet hit the ground by his foot and another went over his head.

Time to go.

Brody howled as he gunned the bike to life.

With a spray of dirt, he took off, trying to spot Layla's white gown in the darkness shrouding the land around the ramshackle house and garage.

Nothing.

The bark of dogs, as they woke to the chaos, led him to believe one of two things. Either, one, Layla was already back in custody and unable to control them, or, two, she'd booked it.

He wagered on the second.

Given he could hear revving engines— more bikes stashed somewhere on the property about to give chase—he needed to choose a direction. He sniffed for options and came up with a pair of possible plans. A, He could follow the faint trail of cinnamon and the woman he didn't know what to think of, or, B, He could go off in a different direction and hope that, by splitting the enemy he'd improve his chances on making it to either a phone or help.

Reid really needed an update on the situation. The girl would only slow him down. He could return later to rescue her. *And take her home with us.*

To contain her power.

To keep her.

So she couldn't be used against them.

But she could totally use me. Naked.

Naked Layla meant he thought of the hooded dude's sick plans for her. He wanted her pregnant. By any means.

Brody could only assume he hoped to breed her power, to create a more malleable tool for his use. Sick. Unacceptable. What if he didn't make it back in time to prevent it?

He followed cinnamon.

Alone, naked and without even a bloody gun, or a pair of pants, Brody went after the woman with the exotic scent.

I'm coming to rescue you, sweetheart.

But when he found her, she seemed less than pleased.

Chapter Ten

Stupid wolf shifter with his bloody sharp nose. Layla should have known he'd track her, even if he rode a noisy dirt bike spitting out fumes.

She'd opted to not have her flying minions attack him, not that they were doing much good with those following.

Tiny bodies against big swiping hands, along with those on foot not afraid to spray buckshot, meant her mini army didn't last long. Mental orders couldn't prevail against self-preservation. Off her surviving bats went in search of shelter and easier prey.

Damn. With them gone, it didn't leave her with much to attack Brody when he skidded to a halt beside her.

Naked.

On a bike.

Did she mention he was gloriously naked?

The warmth infusing her body pushed back the cold, creeping dampness of the woods.

"Get on. We're going for a ride."

Mmm. Ride. Brody. Naked.

Given the crude language she'd found herself exposed to for the last few years, was it any wonder her first thought didn't involve the bike?

He repeated himself. "Whatever's got you mooning, snap out of it, sweetheart. We've got to go, so get your luscious butt on the back of this bike. The enemy is not far behind me. We need to make some tracks."

He wants me to sit where? She looked at the tiny wedge of seat left behind him. Why, she'd practically have to wrap all her limbs around his nude torso and have her crotch pressed against his firm buttocks. Her arms locked around his muscled chest. So close. Not a good idea. "No."

"This isn't the time to argue. Get on."

"How about, instead, you lead them off that way while I go this way?" she said, pointing in opposite directions.

"They are right on our tail, Bait. Or is it your plan to get caught again just because you don't want to come with me to Kodiak Point?"

"To face your alpha."

"Probably."

"And maybe get jailed or worse."

To his credit he didn't lie. "I doubt it will come to that once he hears your story."

"Not good enough."

"Why must you make everything so hard?" he growled.

Why did she? Layla couldn't have said, but she also knew his plan was probably not in her best interest. Trade one prison for another? No thank you.

"Deal with it." With those words, she sprinted away, choosing the toughest terrain for him to follow, barreling through the densest underbrush. Thing was, her mad dash sprint left a clear trail.

Brody paralleled her, shouting occasionally. "You're tiring yourself for nothing."

Not nothing. Freedom.

"They're going to catch you."

Not without an epic fight. She was beginning to feel the spark that signaled animal consciousness. Perhaps enough to keep those chasing from nabbing her.

And by them, did she include Brody in that group?

He seemed determined to stick with her. He swerved in close. "Get on."

"No."

"I'm going to spank you later for this."

"I'll make spiders crawl up your nose."

She could do a lot worse, but for some reason, she couldn't bring herself to threaten him with it.

"That is fucking disturbing to know."

"Then leave me alone."

"Dammit, sweetheart. I'm trying to rescue you here. Why—"

The rest of his words got lost as the first of their pursuers finally caught up to them, the loud rumble of their motors drowning all sound.

Still running, Layla ignored Brody and focused on her own survival, casting out her senses to have the wildlife she could mentally touch report on the situation around her.

She should have focused more on the

ground.

Her foot hooked an exposed root, and *wham*, she met the less than forgiving surface of the forest floor. It was not a gentle hello.

Before she could scramble to her feet, a dirt bike shot past her, but not far before it spun around. Despite the gloom, she could tell by the leer the driver bore, and the fact he wore clothes, that she didn't face Brody.

Not good!

She shot to her feet and cast out a mental call for help to no avail. The wildlife here was too small and timid even for such a frantic command. They squeaked in their dens, they shivered in fear, and she backed away from the leering guy, who ditched his bike to come at her on foot.

He never laid a hand on her. Focused on the unfolding event in front of her, she never noted another dirt bike had gotten close. It shot from the side, and she gaped as the rider—naked and riveting in the scant starlight—clotheslined her attacker with a yodeled, "Yee-fucking-haw!"

The naked cowboy on his metal horse hit the ground, miraculously still seated on his bike, and spun. This time when Brody shouted, "Get the fuck on," she obeyed.

There was pride and determination, and then there was stupidity. *I don't want to be that girl in the book who rejects common sense.*

Survival was more important.

Straddling the bike was just as awkward and uncomfortable as expected. The sliver of seat barely cupped her bottom, which meant she had to clamp her thighs around Brody, wrap her arms around his chest, and lean her cheek against the skin of shoulder.

"Hold on, sweetheart."

I am, and liking it way too much.

Or she was for a few seconds, and then thrill-fueled terror took hold of her as Brody shot off into the darkness, the bike straining with the addition of her body weight but still moving them faster and farther than she could have managed on foot.

Maybe they could escape. There was just one problem, namely, Brody headed away from the nearest town, not toward it.

"You're going the wrong way," she shouted, her assertion just barely carrying over the sound of the engine and wind whipping the words away as soon as she uttered them.

"No, I'm not. Home is west."

"But supplies are southeast."

"We're going home."

She bit her tongue for the moment. Having an argument on a bike probably wasn't the smartest idea, especially since they still had determined pursuers.

A four-wheeler came crashing from the bushes, with a driver channeling his inner daredevil and a passenger toting a shotgun.

"Shit!" Brody cursed as he leaned them to one side, his foot bracing their sharp turn away from the weapon.

Boom.

The shot gun fired, and she closed her eyes

tight, waiting for the stinging pain.

Missed.

But their pursuers seemed determined to try again. Brody weaved and dipped while she held on for dear life, his crazy speed and antics making her determined not to fall off, especially not on this rocky terrain.

Terrain that conspired against them. The ground, all of a sudden, inclined sharply, too sharply for the bike. Brody skidded to a halt and turned, practically tossing her off.

He gunned the motor as he eyed the shadowy forest behind them, the hum of other engines loud, which meant they were close.

"What are you waiting for?"

"My opening."

Three vehicles emerged from the concealment of the trees, the flash of the drivers' eyes ominous pinpricks of color. At least to her.

Usually she didn't fear feral animals. But these wild shifters, ones not bound by laws, didn't obey her commands, and she didn't have the master here to temper their violent nature.

Would they show care when they dragged her back to meet her punishment?

If we go back.

Brody had shown himself resourceful thus far. Perhaps he'd slip this noose.

Again, he gunned the bike. "Hold on tight. We're going to have to squeeze this."

But then Lady Luck showed her bitchy side again.

The engine coughed. Choked. Then died.

Even she winced as one of their pursuers laughed and said, "For once I'm glad Tommy's a lazy prick who never thinks to fill his tank."

Tommy was taken off her Christmas list. Because of him, they now no longer had wheels.

"Get off the bike nice and slow with your hands up," ordered the guy on the four-wheeler. His pal on the back aimed his shotgun in their direction.

No point in fighting the inevitable. Layla slid off the dirt bike and immediately felt a pang at the loss of Brody's body heat. She stood beside him, hands held up in surrender.

Brody, on the other hand, didn't move.

"I said get off the bike." The fellow held out a familiar remote and jabbed the button.

Nothing happened. The guy slapped it. Banged it off his handlebars, cursed a few times, but the little box wouldn't work.

"Fucking Tommy didn't change the batteries," he muttered with disgust.

Tommy was re-added to her Christmas list.

"Ah, is your little toy not working?" taunted Brody, with no sense of preservation.

It impressed her a bit, especially given the odds. She also wondered at his mental state, because really, who did that with these odds?

"Don't piss me off, wolf boy. Get off the bike and put your hands in the air."

"Make me." No doubting the challenge there.

She stared at the sky while she tapped her foot, waiting for the game of testosterone chicken to play its course.

"The master said to bring you back. He never said we couldn't hurt you, dog."

"Again, I'd like to see you try. But since you're more interested in talking, I've got something to say. Five."

"What the fuck is that supposed to mean?"

"Four."

"Stop screwing around."

"Three."

"Shoot him." The guy with the shotgun aimed then cursed as he realized he'd not primed his weapon. The other guys on the bikes ditched their rides and fumbled for their weapons.

Brody smiled. "Two."

"What are you waiting for? Shoot—"

She never heard the one. Instead, the dirt bike Brody straddled went toppling to the opposite side of her as Brody sprang from it, morphing into a mighty wolf, a timber wolf with striated black, silver, and white fur.

Savage grace in motion that took out the screaming fellow before the guy with the shotgun managed to reload. The other guys weren't as ill prepared. They'd managed to pull free their weapons, and she noted the muzzle flashes and her ears rang from the cracks as they fired at the wolf determined to bring them down.

Yet, somehow, they kept missing Brody as he moved in a jagged fashion that just allowed him to avoid getting shot each time.

Unfortunately, they had numbers on their side, which, given the approaching shouts, were about to swell.

Brody seemed to not like the turn of events. He bounded back in her direction then up the embankment at her back.

She craned to watch him, saw him incline his shaggy head her way as if to say, "You coming?"

Oh, what the hell. Why not? Might as well make escape fifty-seven memorable. They'd come this far, why not go a few more yards?

The rough surface of the stones scraped at her feet, but given she only got to wear shoes when the weather turned nasty, she barely noted it. She did, however, envy Brody's padded paws, which allowed him to bound and clamber effortlessly the sharper than expected incline.

Not exactly the most comfortable escape. It didn't help that the occasional shot pinged off the stony surface, sending hard flecks splattering. Ouch.

The random shots didn't last long, as someone shouted, "You fucking idiot, stop shooting. If we accidentally kill the girl, the master will rip out our intestines and feed them to us, like he did with poor Jory."

Poor Jory, indeed. He'd nicked her with a bullet during escape fifty-three. Came close to an artery, too. His screams echoed for miles around as master made an example of his ineptitude.

The shooting halted, and with only the worry of those climbing below them to distract her, Layla made better time, even if she now leaned forward and had to use her fingers to grip and help pull herself up.

Until a set of strong hands grabbed her by the wrists and yanked.

"Eep!"

She couldn't help her startled yell as a suddenly human again Brody hauled her to the top of the rocky mountain. Okay, more like a hill, but given how she panted and her muscles complained, it seemed a lot bigger.

He didn't waste time asking how she was— some rescuer he was turning out to be. He didn't say anything as he tugged her away from the edge, but not as far as she would have liked, probably on account of the cliff on the other side.

Trapped between a suicidal drop and rabid master's minions. Escape fifty-seven truly was determined to make itself memorable.

"Can you swim?" he asked as she tried to back away from the sheared-off embankment.

"Nope. And I don't think now's the time to learn."

"We don't have much of a choice. It's either jump or go back to jail."

"I can't drown in prison."

"I wouldn't let you sink."

"Answer is still no," she replied, not even trying to stem the shudder of the memory from the last time she'd ended up in water over her head. How clearly she recalled the panic and fear as her lungs burned for oxygen before her head bobbed to the surface. She'd gotten lucky that time.

Judging by the ominous slick look of the water coursing below, she didn't think it would prove as friendly as the shallow lake she fell in during escape twenty-one.

"I'll stall them while you escape," she offered, turning away and raising her hands in surrender.

"Like fuck," was the only growled warning she got before he wrapped an arm around her waist and leaped over the edge.

Wind whistled as they shot down.

Splash.

They hit the cold river, and she couldn't help but scream. Bad idea.

Water in my eyes. My mouth. Help!

She couldn't help the panic as she sank.

She didn't sink far.

Fingers fisted her hair and yanked painfully, popping her head into the air, where she choked and sputtered.

And flailed.

"Calm down, sweetheart, I've got you. I won't let you sink." Brody tried to calm her. He also kept his word.

She didn't sink, or drown, but that didn't mean she forgave him when he eventually dragged her soaked and exhausted—and very prune-like—body to shore.

Chapter Eleven

The fly landed on his nose again, its accuracy in being a pest spot-on. Brody swatted his hand at it, and it buzzed off indignantly, only to return. It perched right on the tip of his nose, and he practically went cross-eyed glaring at it.

Damned pest!

A sound came from his left. He shot Layla a look. Indeed, she was snickering.

Not bad enough he was naked, trudging through the woods, his feet sore from the abuse when he'd used them with the bike. She had to mock him on top of it?

He frowned as the fly once again landed with unerring accuracy on his nose, taunting him. It was unnatural. "Are you the one doing this?" he asked.

A coy smile curved her lips. "Maybe."

Which meant yes. "Stop it."

"What if I don't want to?"

"You will cease at once."

She tapped her chin as if in thought. Her dark locks flew as she shook her head. "No."

"What do you mean no? This is not a democracy. I'm in charge of this escape. You will obey." Yeah, he told her. Problem was, she didn't seem intent on listening. No respect.

"First off, you would have never escaped without my help and second…" A pink tongue emerged from lips he'd kissed and blew wetly at him.

The childish reply stunned him for a moment. "You did not just do that."

"I did. And I'm also doing this." She flashed him a middle finger, along with a smirk. "I've had time to think over our situation, and I've decided you're a jerk."

"I'm a jerk? I'm not the one siccing bacteria-laden flies at you."

"You deserve it. You made me think I could trust you."

"Who says you can't?"

"You threw me off a cliff, into a raging river, knowing I couldn't swim."

"To save your life."

"Ha, it wasn't my life in danger. Those idiots wouldn't have hurt me. They wouldn't have dared."

"So you'd prefer to return to captivity than escape?"

"Funny you should mention that. I was escaping just fine on my own before you arrived like a rabid psycho on a bike to muck things up."

He ogled her. "Just fine? When I showed up, you were like a deer in headlights facing down a hired killer."

Her chin tilted at a stubborn angle. "I would have handled it."

"With what? A swarm of mosquitos?"

"Actually, I had a line on a wasps' nest when you interrupted."

"Wasps against a killer?" He shook his head. "Shit like that is why I can't let you wander around alone."

"Why? Because I'm a girl and I just might be able to take care of myself?"

"No, because you're an idiot who thinks she can. So far if you ask me, you've been lucky. Your worth to the hooded fellow is what's made these guys hold back. You might not always be able to count on that."

"What makes you any better than them? After all, aren't you doing the same thing by taking me to this Reid guy?"

"Because he's alpha at Kodiak Point."

"So what? A prisoner to an alpha, or a prisoner to some other guy, I don't see the difference."

"You're not a prisoner." Not exactly.

"Says the guy who kidnapped me when I was trying to escape."

"For your own good. You do want to avoid capture, right?"

She rolled her eyes. "Well, duh. But I don't need you for that."

Irritation built as she kept denying her need of him. *She needs me, whether she likes it or not.* "Despite your skills with wildlife, you wouldn't last out here on your own, and you know it." He didn't need the dirty look she shot his way to know he'd put his paw in his mouth.

"I bet you I could. Let me go and I'll prove it."

"No."

"Why not?"

"Because you're too dangerous to let wander about by yourself."

She stopped short and stared at him. "Hold on. Just a minute ago, I was too inept to be on my own, and now I'm too dangerous? That makes no sense."

Nope, just like his attraction to her didn't. Annoying him or not, he couldn't help but want her. And hiding it was about to get difficult.

He dropped his hands and turned away to resume walking. "Being dangerous doesn't mean you'd survive. There are all kinds of things out here that could kill you. You need me."

"You're an ass."

"If you're implying I'm stubborn then yes. I am."

Now it was her turn to go cross-eyed. "You do know there's enough animal life around here that I could probably start a stampede and squish your stubborn carcass to death."

"But you won't."

She scowled. "But I could."

"But you won't."

"What makes you think that?"

Because he could smell it. Irritated with him or not, she wanted him, and the perfume of her arousal was driving him nuts, almost as nuts as her verbal arguing.

When talk was getting a man nowhere, it

was time to resort to a more hands-on approach. It had also been much too long since he'd last touched her. He could wait no longer.

He dragged her into his arms and kissed her. Over and over.

When he finally let her breathe on her own, her pulse raced, a flush tinted her cheeks, and her eyes smoldered like purple fire. "I hate you."

"Hate me all you want, but you have to admit I'm a great kisser."

"I wouldn't know. I've never kissed another man."

And she never would.

Ack, there he went with those possessive thoughts again.

"You'll be sorely disappointed if you do. I am the best." Modesty had no place when a man boasted of his prowess.

"What a cocky statement. And is that a dare I hear? You know what, on second thought, we should go to your hometown. It's time I got to mingle with more people. More men. Maybe get a basis of comparison when it comes to kissing technique. How many men do you think I need to smooch to get a proper idea? Three, five, ten?" She smiled mockingly. Her gaze challenged.

He knew she did on purpose to goad him. Knew it and yet…

Jealousy burned fast and hot.

"You will kiss no others!" He practically roared the order at her, loud enough that she gaped at him.

She planted her hands on her hips and

leaned toward him. "You can't stop me. I'll kiss whomever I damned well please. *And*," she smirked, "I'll like it."

You will not.

Once again, he lost control, or never had it to begin with. He dragged her into his arms and slanted his mouth over hers, possessing it with a fierce passion he'd never felt for another woman.

One brief, torrid taste. She broke the embrace and stared at him, panting slightly. Her lips moved, forming words that took a moment to filter. "Stop that."

Stop kissing her? Why would he do that when he could see the smoldering interest in her eyes? Smell her arousal.

Need her. Now.

With no conscious thought, he placed his big hands on her waist, her flared waist covered only by that stupid flimsy gown, which was little more than a rag since their dip in the river.

He hoisted her until her lips were but a hairsbreadth away. For once, she didn't speak. Didn't harangue. She stared at him, eyes wide, lips parted. Utterly tempting.

He kissed her again, taking his time exploring her mouth. Truly tasting her, her hesitance, tinged with hunger. A crack of a branch had her breaking off the embrace.

"We shouldn't do this."

"Why?"

"We're out in the open. Someone will see."

"There's no one around for miles, and you know it." They'd traveled miles in the river, bobbing like flotsam, far enough to make pursuit difficult.

"We don't have time for this," she said, her voice soft and breathy.

He begged to differ. It wouldn't take long. Not with the way their passion burned bright.

"I'm making time." Because he just might explode if he didn't. The lack of control bothered him on some level, but common sense was overpowered by need.

Desire.

Want.

A primal want that would let nothing stand in its way.

Once more, he dipped in to take her lips, claiming what was his. *Mine. She's mine. All mine.*

Admitting, even if only in his mind, transformed the caress. It went from gentle to fiery and possessive. She no longer protested, and he would have kissed her breathless if she did. There was no turning back. He needed this woman. Needed her and he would have her. Not just now, but forever.

And ever.

Oh shit. I'm a goner.

In that moment, with that one thought, he knew he'd just kissed the bachelor life goodbye. No matter what happened next, it would involve this woman.

His mate.

Mine.

Now he just had to convince her of that fact.

At first, she held herself stiffly in his grasp, but as his lips covered over, nibbling and teasing, she relaxed. She kissed him back, her tentative nips of his lip making an already turgid situation even harder.

He knew he'd achieved true capitulation when she draped her arms around his neck. He squeezed her, and she gasped, a sound he swallowed as she opened her mouth. He didn't waste the chance and slid his tongue within the warm recess of her mouth.

How could the taste of her, cinnamon-sweet, drive him so utterly mad with desire?

Primal need pushed him. Instinct drove him. His wolf, usually a silent passenger, begged him to mark her. Claim her.

Utter insanity. Or the mating fever his father once warned him about. It didn't strike everyone, just those who proved most stubborn. And when it hit…

"You are but just a bobbing cork in a sea of rough waters, buoyed by her presence, yet cast adrift with no steady footing." Just one of his dad's many quirky explanations for the basic tenets of life.

No matter their short acquaintance, his being recognized her as the one, and Brody wasn't one to argue with fate, at least not the pleasurable kind.

He still held her suspended in the air, which meant he couldn't let his hands rove her curvaceous body, and he so craved a touch. Yet putting her down meant craning because she was much shorter than him. He had a simpler solution.

"Put your legs around my waist," he murmured against her lips. For a moment, he feared she'd protest, but it seemed the fever racing through him had infected her too. Her limbs wrapped around his frame, and he sank down to the ground, the moss patch spongy and cool against his hot skin. It didn't cool his ardor in the least, probably because the new position had her straddling him and kissing him while her fingers dug into the hair at his nape, weaving and tugging, as her trepidations melted and desire consumed her.

Oh, how her lust enflamed her, emboldening her so that her tongue forayed into his mouth, tangling with his own.

Brody was a man of experience, and he'd kissed his fair share of woman, but none had ever ignited him like Layla did. None made him want to forget the niceties of foreplay and just slide himself into her, pounding until they both found release.

But he retained some measure of sanity, the barest control. With her inexperience, he had to take care, lest he frighten her, or hurt her, both things he couldn't allow. But it was hard holding back, especially since her sex, covered only in the thinnest of cotton, pressed against his groin, leaving him wet as her arousal soaked through the fabric and the heat scorched.

With them seated, he no longer needed to hold her, which meant his hands could leave the indent of her waist and cup the roundness of her ass. Once again, her damned gown got between him and his goal. He couldn't help a low growl as he slid the fabric out of the way until he could slip his fingers past the elastic waistband of her underpants.

Smooth flesh. Full cheeks. Perfection.

He squeezed the perfect globes, and she squirmed atop him and emitted a gasp against his lips. The tiny sound thrilled him, but not as much as the fact she pressed herself tighter to him. Their teeth clanged as she ground herself impatiently against his body, the fullness of her breasts pressing against his chest, her nipples hard points that prodded.

They're begging for my mouth.

They were. He could tell. And he wasn't a man to deny a plea like that.

It took but a moment to tug the gown she wore up and overhead, tossing it aside, leaving her clad only in panties. He'd remove those in a bit, but for the moment, he was riveted by her breasts.

More than a handful, they hung a touch heavy, giving them a delightful curve to cup, which he did. With her dusky skin, he was surprised at how pink the nipples were. He'd expected a darker hue, but the rosebuds were a delight, and as he stared at them—practically drooling—they tightened into little nubs. He couldn't resist stroking the pad of his thumb over one. A tremor shook her at his calloused touch.

He stroked again and was rewarded with an even bigger shudder. Eager for more, he let his free hand palm the middle of her back, arching her away from him to better display her breasts. It also made her nipples, those tasty-looking buds, protrude. He could resist no longer. He latched on to one, delighting in her soft cry.

The heat of her sex and the dampness increased, a visible sign of her enjoyment, not that he needed it, not with the way she clutched at his head and cried out with each suck and tug of his mouth.

Not one to neglect, he switched to the other breast, spurred on by her sounds of pleasure and his own delight in the perfection of her plump breasts.

Bountiful and soft. Unlike some of the more athletic women he'd been with, Layla's breasts had natural cushiness to them. Pillowy enough for a man's head. He buried his face against her flesh, reveling in the silkiness of her skin. The deep valley between them brought to mind erotic images of him sliding his cock between them, the tip of his erection prodding at her full lips.

His turn to shudder.

"Brody." She sighed his name. Her body shuddered at his touch. Her sweet sex continued to heat and seep honey against him.

He could wait no longer. He had to have her. Needed to sink into the velvety heat that awaited him.

It took only a tug to rip the panties from her body. Then she was pressed against him.

Wet flesh against his turgid cock. The moisture of her arousal covered him, and it was his turn to shudder.

"Lift yourself just a bit, sweetheart," he murmured.

She obeyed, lifting her body on her knees so that her sex was poised above his cock, which bobbed forward, seeking the source of heat.

He guided the tip of his dick to her sex, probing her and hearing her exclaim as he dragged the head back and forth against her.

She trembled.

So did he.

He wrapped one arm around her waist while his other hand guided his shaft into the warmth of her body.

The barrier he soon encountered took him a moment to comprehend. He understood what it meant. He'd more or less expected it after her claim she'd never kissed another, but to feel the actual proof, to have it stand in his way?

Mine. Only mine. Untouched by none other. His.

He couldn't have described all the emotions suddenly coursing through him, but the strongest one of all was thanks. Thanks he'd found this woman. Thanks she'd waited until this moment to gift her most precious of gifts. But he also had some regret because such a precious thing deserved better than a forest floor, on the run, and exhausted from escape.

Too late to stop now.

He thrust up as he pushed her down, tearing through her innocence, knowing swift was better than prolonged.

She cried out and recoiled, not far though, as he held her firmly anchored.

For a moment, he didn't move. He let her

adjust to his size and get over the shock of losing her maidenhead.

He captured her lips while he waited, stoking the flames of her passion, relaxing only when she began to respond again. He cupped a breast as he kissed her, stroking his thumb over the tip until her body began to rock. Intentional or not, the motion drew him deeper into her body.

So deep into that tight cavern.

So warm inside her sex.

So fucking incredible, he fought to hold on.

Her rocking motions took on some speed and strength as she pushed down against him, grinding and squeezing and taking and…

Thank god, coming!

Her muscles spasmed around his cock, and he let go with a rumbling growl of satisfaction. He let his seed mark her womb, something he'd never done to a woman before.

He made her his. Placed his claim.

It was an intense moment. But as the scent of blood mixed with passion tickled his nose, being a man, he of course ruined the moment.

Chapter Twelve

"I can't believe you didn't tell me you were a virgin."

"I can't believe you didn't figure it out," was her tart reply, tart because she was basking in the glow of her first time and he just had to ruin it.

"I guess I knew. I just didn't really know, know until you know, we um—"

"Had sex? For a smart guy you're awfully dumb," she retorted as she tried to move away, but he wouldn't let her go. He kept her seated on his lap, his arms wrapped around her, locking her in place. His shaft, while it had softened since his release, remained within her, a thick reminder of what they'd just done.

As if she could forget. Her own flesh pulsed still, the force of her climax not as easily quelled.

"You say the sweetest things," was his dry response.

"Says the guy who still calls me Bait."

Far from unabashed, he grinned. "You have to admit you are a tempting morsel to dangle in front of a man."

Pleasure blossomed at his compliment. "I hate you." She said it by rote, but it didn't hold any heat.

"You know what they say about that. It's akin to love."

"Love?" She snorted. What an odd word to bring up. "Love is something for fairy tales and romances."

"You don't believe in it?"

"I'd like to, but, in the end, I think self-interest is the stronger emotion."

"I disagree."

"Don't tell me you believe in a forever-after love and soul mates and all that?"

"Of course I believe it."

"Then you're a fool." Layla had seen too much in her lifetime to ever think that the pure love she read about could actually exist. She'd certainly never seen it.

Yet how do you explain your odd emotions where the wolf is concerned?

He was intriguing. Different. He aroused her. It meant nothing. He could leave now, and she would go on her way without looking back.

But I would remember. And why did the thought of him leaving hit her with a sharp pang? Surely she wouldn't miss him? He was annoying and bossy and…still talking.

"Just because some people have hurt you, or broken your trust, doesn't mean everyone will."

"What is it with you and your need for me to trust you?"

"You *can* trust me. I would never do anything to hurt you."

"Then let me go."

"I can't."

Can't. Wouldn't. Because like everyone else, he needed her for an agenda. In his case, to bring her to his clan alpha.

"I know what you're thinking, that I'm doing this to thwart your old captor. But you're wrong. I care for you, Layla."

"Sure you do." She'd heard that lie before. There was only one person who ever truly cared for her and that man, her father, was dead.

"I do. And I'll prove it to you."

"Before or after you deliver me to your alpha? You know what, I don't want to hear your answer." Or his lie. "I'm tired. If we're going to stop moving, then we should get some sleep."

This time when she moved off him, he didn't stop her. She felt his eyes tracking her, though, as she stooped to put on her gown. As for her panties, she doubted the scraps she spotted hanging from a bush were salvageable.

Finding a mossy patch, one that didn't have a sprawled naked man on it, didn't prove hard, but it sure wasn't as comfortable as his lap. She lay down, facing away from him, utterly confused, despite her words to the contrary.

Layla no longer knew what to think. One moment Brody acted as if she was nothing more than his prisoner, a person of interest whom he was bringing to Kodiak Point for questioning, and the next, he made love to her as if she meant something to him. As if he wanted to claim her and keep her and…love her?

What utter nonsense. Layla might have

been a virgin; however, she wasn't gullible.

Falling for her newest captor because he was attractive—and made her body sing with pleasure—was dumb. Worse than dumb, it would hurt her in the end when he betrayed her. Because in the end, didn't everyone betray her?

Her innate power, which everyone wanted to use, made her valuable, but no one ever seemed to realize the skill she wielded resided in a human body rife with human emotions and frailties, such as the ability to get her heart broken.

Did Brody not grasp how his mixed signals toyed with her? On the one hand, he asked her to trust, he showed her he cared. He caressed and said sweet things to her that implied a future. Then, on the other, he reiterated her lack of choice, the danger she posed.

How to reconcile the two?

I should escape. Despite his assertion he'd track and get her back, like he'd already done once, she wasn't convinced. Despite the strange terrain, she would survive because so long as there was life she'd have help.

But the bigger question was, did she want to?

If Brody spoke the truth and this Reid guy who ran the clan in Kodiak Point truly could keep her out of the master's clutches, then should she take the chance and attempt a shot at a normal life? Find a measure of happiness in the small town?

I could give it a try.

But what if it failed?

What if it was just another trap, one she

walked into blindly?

It was hard to imagine the man who'd just caressed her and spoken to her with such earnestness and seeming honesty would betray her. Yet sweet words so easily masked false ones.

Do I really want to go through my entire life never trusting again?

At some point, not everyone was evil. Or so she hoped. But she only had to recall her father's words to wonder.

"Don't ever reveal who you are because even friends will be tempted to use you for their own gain."

She had to wonder over the next few days about that tenet because while Brody asked many things of her—walk where I walk, hold still, kiss me, scream for me—he not once asked her to use her power. Not even to scout for the enemy.

There were none—she knew because she'd commandeered a few avian creatures to act as her eyes in the sky—but she didn't tell him that. She waited for him to ask. Waited for him to order her to bring them dinner or find some shelter or prove she could wield her power over anything in the animal and insect kingdom.

He didn't. Never even alluded to it, leaving her more confused than before.

And, more disturbingly, falling for the wolf.

Despite their lack of equipment, Brody seemed to have no problem getting them where he wanted and supplying them on the way. The man fashioned himself a loincloth of sorts from the vegetation, braiding and twining the fibers. He found them roots they could gnaw on safely, leaves as well. He hunted and built them covered fires, hiding the glow and smoke, and keeping it lit only long enough to cook the meat he hunted.

They never lacked for water because he possessed a knack for always locating a source. He kept her warm after the first night, mostly because every evening, despite her determination to resist, he seduced her then held her cradled in his arms until morning.

Despite her qualms, she loved it.

Even if they didn't have the most basic of amenities and the food situation proved less than ideal, Layla couldn't help but revel in the freedom. It was the longest stint she'd enjoyed in a long while, and when they finally caught sight of the signs of civilization from a bluff, she was almost sorry to see their journey end.

The small settlement they came across didn't boast much, a couple dozen houses and a store, which they had no money for, but it did have a phone, which the guy let Brody borrow to make a few phone calls.

Who wouldn't, given the sad tale Brody weaved.

"The missus and I were honeymooning in the woods, just a minding our business and doing our business if you know what I mean," Brody confided with a wink to the old codger who ran the store. *"When we were attacked by a bear. We managed to get away, but had to leave all our gear behind. We waited a while in the moods until we figured it was safe, but when we tried to go back, well, we kind of got lost. So we started walking south until we found your town."*

The old fellow who owned the place

snickered, but he bought it. He gave them a few supplies and loaned Brody his phone after securing promises of payment.

She assumed he called the alpha of Kodiak Point and other friends, but she didn't bother to eavesdrop. Now that their trek had ended, reality forced its way back in.

What would happen now?

The moment of truth was almost upon them.

Soon she'd find out if the illusion Brody had built would solidify or shatter. *Am I truly free or about to become a prisoner again?*

The owner of the small store offered them the use of a room, not a big space, but it had a twin-sized bed with worn blankets and a pillow, which, after days of moss and leaves, seemed like heaven.

Their host also gave them the use of his bathroom with its shower, which she luxuriated in, the hot water a welcome treat.

She'd dressed in some castoffs and was towel drying her hair when Brody joined her, also freshly showered and dressed in clean clothes. She wondered for a fleeting moment if she should have taken his absence as her chance to flee, but quickly squashed it.

Whatever the future held, she wouldn't run. Yet.

Let's see what happens in Kodiak Point. She'd give the town, and Brody, a chance.

"Members of my clan should be here for us by morning. They're setting out now."

"So we stay here?"

"For the night at least. Then we go home."

Home. Now there was a word she'd like to use.

"And me?" The query emerged soft, questioning. Vulnerable.

"What about you?"

"You spoke to your alpha. What are his plans?" She studied his face closely as he answered, trying to remain alert for any signs of lying or evasion.

His expression betrayed nothing untoward. "I told him I was bringing back a new resident."

"You didn't tell him about my powers?"

"Time enough for that later. I told you. I'm not taking you in as a prisoner. Although…" He shot her a wicked grin. "I wouldn't be averse to holding you down so I could have my way with you." He laughed, a throaty rumble that shot shivers down her spine.

"Why hold me down when I'm willing?" No denying it. He just had to smile at her with the promise of pleasure and her just-donned panties were wet.

"I keep forgetting how innocent you are," he murmured, one step in the small room bringing him into her space.

Sitting on the edge of the bed forced her to peer up at him, that or stare at a rapidly growing part of his anatomy, which bulged the material of his jeans.

"I don't think anyone could call me innocent." She'd seen too much in her life for that.

"In some ways, you are. Like when it comes to lovemaking. There are so many things we've yet to explore. Try. Enjoy…"

Given his position, she could think of something she'd like to try. Something she'd heard of but never attempted. Her hands went to the button and zipper of his pants and undid them.

"What are you doing, sweetheart?"

"Expanding my horizons."

"Are you sure?"

His cock sprang free from the confinement of his pants, long and hard. While she'd seen it before, this close, she truly got to examine it, from the way the head of his shaft formed a big bulb, darker in color than the rest of him. As she watched, the slit at the tip emitted a pearl of liquid. She touched it, rubbed it around his crown, and was gratified to hear him suck in a breath.

"You like that?" A redundant question, but she wanted to hear his answer.

"What do you think?" was his sarcastic retort.

She smiled as she stroked her damp finger down the length of his cock, fascinated by the wide vein, which seemed to pulse the entire way. She gripped him, one hand fisted around his girth, and he let out a low rumble.

It fascinated her how something so rigid, so hard, could feel so soft at the same time, the skin silky. She leaned in for a lick, brushing her tongue against the tip, which had pearled again.

Salty, but not unpleasant. She ran her tongue around the head, lapping it. Again, a low sound came from him, and one of his hands came to rest atop her head, stroking her hair, encouraging her.

Emboldened, she took the tip of him into her mouth and sucked—her actions inspired by the stories she'd read. And now could experience.

His cock twitched in her grip and seemed to grow even plumper. She sucked some more, taking him deeper into her mouth, his thickness just managing to graze past her teeth. He hissed, and when she peeked up at him, wondering if she'd inadvertently caused him injury, she saw him with his head thrown back, eyes shut, and the muscles of his neck strung taut.

A man in the throes of enjoyment, not pain.

It served only to increase her own burgeoning passion and added a bit of fervor to her actions. Her sucking took on a cadence as she bobbed back and forth, her hand maintaining a tight, anchoring grip. His breathing quickened, and while she couldn't hear his heart race, she could feel it in the way the vein in his shaft pulsed, faster and faster. He also began to thrust his hips, timing it with her head bobs, driving himself a little deeper, but not too far. Her hand on his cock made sure of that.

She wondered if she could bring him to release, like he had with her. But Brody had different plans. With a groan, he pulled away from her, leaving her wet mouth with an audible pop, and she made a protesting noise.

"Bring it back," she demanded. "I wasn't done."

"Yeah, but I almost was," he growled. "And that would be too soon for what I want to do."

"Give it to me."

"Oh, I intend to give it to you. Just not quite yet."

He drew her up, high enough to plaster his lips against hers, the fieriness of his kiss dispelling her protest. But a kiss wasn't his only aim. His hands divested her of her clothing. She had no issue with that, not when it meant she got to press her naked skin against his, something she never seemed to tire of. She loved the heat he emitted. Loved the flesh-on-flesh contact. Loved it even when he toppled them on the mattress, the springs making them bounce as they squeaked in alarm.

She couldn't help but giggle. "Think it will hold us?"

"Probably not, but it sure as hell beats getting grass marks on my knees and ass," he jested.

At that, she laughed, a pure sound of mirth that should have seemed out of place given their sexual position and intent yet felt so right. He leaned up on his forearms, and she was able to admire the view, a view she never tired of with his perfect chest, rippled with mouth-watering muscles, defined, wide shoulders, and flat nipples. She reached a hand to touch his smooth skin and dragged her nails lightly from his pecs to the indent of his waist. He sucked in a breath, and his eyes went from smoldering with fire to a glowing golden.

She knew that look. It meant fun times

ahead.

When she would have dragged her hand lower, he trapped it between their bodies. "My turn to play," he said in a husky tone. The promise in his words sent a shudder through her.

But he didn't immediately act. He stared instead, his intent gaze taking in what he could see. Her nipples puckered under his scrutiny, anticipating his attention.

Slowly, too slowly in her impatient mind, he lowered his face until he could brush his lips across her erect nubs. A sigh left Layla as she arched, silently willing him to suck them. He ignored the unspoken plea, but he did other things. Pleasurable things.

The hot flick of his tongue made her cry out. He did it again before circling the very tip of it around her nipple. She moaned at his slow torture, but it didn't stop his slow tease.

She weaved her fingers through his hair and pulled him to her, or tried to. She wanted him to take her engorged nipple into his mouth. It didn't work. He chuckled, his warm breath fluttering over the tips, making them ache even more.

"You're killing me," she groaned, unable to remain silent.

"No worse than what you just did to me, sweetheart."

He blew on her wet nipple, and she bucked, her desire screaming for more. Her grip on his hair tightened, but he wouldn't be forced. And he was the stronger of them. With ease, he untangled her fingers from his hair, only to trap them in his iron grip. He pushed her hands above her head, and no amount of struggling or straining could free them. It was frightening, as it proved her vulnerability to him, but it was also exhilarating because she knew he wouldn't hurt her. On the contrary, without her getting in his way, he continued his lazy exploration of her breasts.

Anticipation thrummed throughout her body so that when he finally took her more than ready nub into his mouth, she couldn't help but yell a little. She might have even had a mini orgasm. Her channel certainly pulsed in pleasure.

Taking his time, his mouth sucked and tugged at her erect nipples. He split his attention between the pair, driving her mindless with sensation.

When he did finally stop his decadent tease, she whimpered then moaned as his mouth took a path south. It dragged over the swell of her stomach. Tickled around her belly button before choosing to trail down her left thigh, the closeness of his mouth to her sex making her almost sob.

She still couldn't grasp him or touch or do anything, as he dragged her trapped hands down as he traveled, placing them on her belly.

He kissed his way to the skin of her inner thigh. Then switched sides.

She could have screamed.

He kissed his way around, soft nibbles, closer and closer and…

This time she did protest. "Stop teasing me!"

"But I'm having fun. And so are you," was

his devilish reply as he blew on her damp sex.

Oh how that made her quiver. Her entire channel clenched, and she could have sobbed when he still didn't give her what she needed.

"Hands over your head," he ordered, and if it meant relief, then she'd obey.

She raised them over her head.

"You might want to grip the headboard," he advised with a wicked smile. He leaned back from her and grabbed his cock. As she watched, his thumb smoothed the clear liquid coming from the tip over the swollen head.

She swallowed but held on tight to the brass headboard.

Hand still holding his shaft, he used his other to run a finger down her moist slit. A shudder went through her, and her breathing came in short pants. Much as she loved his touch, she had to wonder if the anticipation was even more exciting.

"You are so beautiful," he murmured as he leaned forward, and his head ducked between her legs so he could blow hotly on her.

And finally the wait was over.

Wide hands cupped her ass and raised her just enough for him to feast on her sex. She almost came with the first wet stroke of his tongue. She definitely moaned. And groaned and made a whole bevy of sounds as he proceeded to sensually torture her pussy.

Flicks of his tongue against her clit made her cry out. His tongue running circles around the bundle of nerves had her panting. The jab of it between her wet folds made her whimper. So many different erotic sensations, all leading to one giant culmination. But as blissful as all his actions were, he never quite let her go off the edge and orgasm. He held off just enough. Teased her to within screaming distance.

He forced her to beg. "Please."

His reply? "Not yet."

She could have cried from need.

He did take some pity on her, though. He let go of her ass and let her sink back on to the mattress, but only because he required a hand. Fingers stroked across her slick slit, stroked, touched, and then thrust in. Oh my. His finger penetrated her sex, pumping in and out, but it wasn't thick enough to satisfy, not when she knew what he felt like.

She closed her eyes as she gyrated her hips in time to his finger thrusts. Thus she didn't notice his positioning of his body until the digit pulled free and the swollen head of his cock butted against her. He rubbed the tip against her moist core, teasing her with its size. Teasing her with the pleasure she knew would come.

Inch by inch, he inserted himself, slowly, oh so slowly, stretching her channel, filling her deliciously. Her sex spasmed around him, and he groaned.

"Hold on just a little bit longer," he urged.

She'd try, but she sat on the edge of ecstasy. It wouldn't take much to shove her off.

Especially if he thought to torture her some more. But it seemed his teasing was done. Once fully seated, he began to thrust. Pump. His pace starting out slow, but quickly transitioning until he pistoned into her, each stroke striking deep, heightening her pleasure until it almost hurt. She tightened, and she almost forgot to breathe.

Right there. Almost. Almost.

Even though she didn't speak, he understood she was on the cusp. His penetrating jabs got more forceful. She was past moans, and he was no longer giving commands, probably because he panted harshly as he pistoned. Even without words, their pleasure play was anything but quiet. Flesh slapped on flesh.

Harder.

Faster.

Deeper.

Her body arched off the mattress, bowing as her orgasm finally struck. A deep shudder went through her, again and again as wave after wave of bliss rolled through her.

She didn't come alone. Brody roared one word that sounded suspiciously like "Mine!" before spurting hotly inside her.

And then collapsing. But not because of exhaustion.

It seemed in their mindless need for one another, they'd both neglected one important thing. A fatal mistake. They'd thought themselves safe.

Wrong.

Escape fifty-seven had just come to an end.

Chapter Thirteen

Reality, a cold bitch with no care for lovers, intruded on the intimate moment, and Brody could have killed her.

Such a glorious joining of bodies—and souls—didn't deserve such an ignoble end, but the darts in his ass said otherwise.

It was his own fault.

I should have known better.

He'd thought them safe at least for the night. He could have sworn no one trailed them and that his southern path would mislead their pursuers who would expect them to head due west to the safety of his clan. Or at least a town where he could hitch a ride.

While they did need wheels and most especially a phone so he could call in, of more import was making sure they weren't recaptured, hence his arrival in the small hamlet. The spare room offered to them by the shopkeeper in town was a bonus.

But complacency was his enemy.

The dude who called himself the master had found them, or at least his minions had because

Brody recognized the guy who stood inside the door with the tranq gun in hand. Although, he'd initially squashed Layla at the impact of the darts, his first impulse being to shield her body, now that he realized they weren't firing bullets, Brody rolled off Layla, prepared to kill the fucker. At least that was his plan, were it not for the half-dozen darts shot into his upper torso.

Unlike the ones in his ass, Brody ripped them out and flung them to the side as he staggered to his feet, placing himself between the attackers and a groggy Layla, who'd gotten hit with a pair of tufted missiles.

Her "What's going on?" emerged slurred.

"We've got company," he growled, a head shake doing nothing about the effects of the tranquilizers, which were already slowing his movements and speech down.

"No," she whispered, echoing his own thoughts. "But how? How did they find us?"

The how didn't matter. It was how they would escape that did. Already swaying on his feet, Brody had only moments before he would succumb to the drugs working on his system. He couldn't allow that to happen because, if he passed out, he'd leave Layla defenseless.

I won't let her go back to that prick. I won't.

He called to his beast side, but his wolf was too drowsy, the sedatives already at work.

The puffing sound of more darts firing made him brace for impact, but the target wasn't Brody but his woman, whose hair had begun to rise in a static halo, a sign of her drawing on her power.

Yeah, sweetheart, call forth your furry minions.

Too late.

Her eyes fluttered.

Then shut.

Brody let out a bellow, rage-filled and anguished. This couldn't be happening. Not this close to freedom and aid. *Not after I promised her she wouldn't ever have to go back. Not after realizing how much she means to me.*

Barreling forward, he reached out to grab the prick with the dart gun, but his limbs wouldn't cooperate, and his muscles went limp. For a moment he could grasp why men relied on erectile remedies. Nothing worse than the body not responding when commanded.

Work, damn you. Obey me, body.

Nope.

He sank to his knees then pitched forward.

Blackness hovered, even though he snarled at it to get back. It proved relentless. His senses dulled. Through the invisible cotton clogging his ears, he thought he heard yells. The rumble of a bear. Then he blinked, the longest blink ever, and when he opened his eyes again, he let out an unmanly yelp.

No. Not this. Anything but this. It seemed he'd gone from one frying pan of a situation to another.

Brown eyes peered at him. Familiar ones to go with the voice saying, "Hey, Brody, I like the artwork you got on your ass. I hope you don't mind, but I took a picture and sent it to my tattoo artist."

A pink bunny with pin-up-girl cleavage and a sassy wink, a reminder of his military days where he learned to never pass out with his buddies in a hole of a bar downtown.

"Don't make me kill you, Travis," Brody mumbled as he moved to a sitting position, still naked but no longer in the small bedroom he'd shared with Layla.

Judging by the scrapes on his legs, someone had dragged him, but not too far because he recognized the interior of the general store.

"What happened?" he asked.

"You got jumped, old man."

Duh. Trust the younger grizzly to point out the obvious.

As the effects of the drug cleared, Brody peered around, taking in the signs of violence. Of more import than the damage they'd caused, where was his woman?

"Where's Layla?"

"Who?"

"The girl I was with. Long hair. Tanned skin." Hot body and most important thing to him right now. "Where is she?" Why couldn't he scent her?

"Sorry, dude. There was no chick when we got here. Just a few scrawny dudes trying to lug your carcass across the floor. Bunch of pussies couldn't even lift you. I assumed you wouldn't want to go with them, so I grizzlied their asses." Travis beamed, which to those who didn't know him meant a shit-eating grin that stretched from ear to ear and invited more than one fist to wipe it.

"I'm afraid to ask what that means."

"I took them out of course."

"More like bashed their skulls together," rumbled another familiar voice. Boris appeared, looking as ornery as ever, and totally welcome. If the moose was around, then Brody was safe from everyone but idiots.

"Hey, not all of us think it's appropriate to tear the limbs off our opponents to use them as clubs."

"Then you're missing all the fun," Boris replied with an evil grin.

"Doesn't Jan get pissed at all the bloody laundry you must make?"

"My mate usually cheers me on when I get all badass. And when the rack comes out…" The smug smile on Boris' face said it all.

"What is it about chicks digging the horns?" Travis complained. "I don't get it."

"They're called antlers. And the women dig them because they're majestic."

"And make great coat racks." Travis ducked just in time. The fist aimed his way only brushed the top of his head.

It didn't curb his tongue. "Getting slow, old man."

Whack. The punch Boris followed up with connected, and Travis staggered. Boris snorted. "Old? Ha. It's called a sucker punch, the oldest trick in the book."

Yay for Brody, the cavalry—with its nonstop rivalry—had arrived. Boris, the deadliest moose you never wanted to meet, was here with everyone's most annoying sidekick, Travis.

Poor kid. Despite his mid-twenties age, he kept trying to be one of the guys, but he'd not gotten exposed to the bonding time the rest of them had during their stint in the military. His lack of experience, though, didn't stop him from tagging along—and for the most part, they let him. Like a younger kid brother, Travis took the brunt of the ribbing and blows. Tough love. But Travis didn't seem to mind because the cub always popped back up smiling.

However, his sense of humor could become grating. Like now when Brody was stressed about Layla's disappearance.

While usually Brody would participate in taking Travis down a notch or two—under the guise of teaching him—he kind of had more pressing matters to deal with such as, "Can we get back on track here and discuss the dudes you head-knocked? What did you do with them after you dropped their asses?"

"Took them prisoner, of course."

Prisoners who liked to commit suicide. "Make sure you keep their mouths open—"

"I know," interrupted Boris. "Don't forget I was there when the first ones we caught bit their bullet. I've got our little friends gagged with a stick so they can't chomp down until the doc gets here. Once she removes the problem teeth, we'll question them."

"What do you mean when she gets here? Wasn't she with you guys?"

Travis shook his head. "Nah. Reid and the

others are still on their way. You just lucked out Boris and I were in the area."

"We were looking for your hairy ass," Boris added.

"Although, now that I've seen it, I have to admit there wasn't as much fur as expected." Travis noted. "Do you shave?"

No, but Brody could glare.

"Smooth naturally?" Travis whistled. "You lucky bastard. Anyhow, we showed up just in time apparently. What happened? Of all the guys, you're one of the last ones I would have expected to see surprised by an ambush. Did they distract you with some local pussy so they could take you out?"

"Kind of. Except Layla's not a local girl. She was a prisoner of the douchebag who has been bugging our town."

"Don't tell me you fell for her story of being a prisoner?" Boris grunted in derision. "More like the bait that almost led to your capture until we came along."

"Yeah, well, she started out as bait, but then it turns out she didn't have a choice and…" Brody trailed off. "You know what, it's fucking complicated, and I don't have time to explain it now. Not when they're getting away with Layla. How much of a head start do they have?"

Travis and Boris shared a look that Brody didn't like.

Given the number of darts Brody was hit with, how long had he slumbered? "What time is it?"

"Just past dawn."

The knowledge he'd been out for a few hours hit him like a fist to the gut. "Oh shit. We've got to get moving. They've got a huge lead on us then."

"We ain't going nowhere until Reid and the others get here."

"I can't wait that long. Once he gets his hands on her, who knows what he'll do to her. Or where he'll take her."

"Why does it matter?"

Why? Why! Was Boris seriously asking him that? Wasn't it fucking obvious? "Because I fucking love her, that's why."

Well, that certainly shut the cavalry up. Boris gaped at him. Travis ogled him. And Brody, yeah, Brody wished he had some pants because using the L word while naked in front of a bunch of guys was just uncool.

"How the fuck did that happen?" Boris asked.

"Gee, I don't know. I met her. We clicked. She's my woman. Does it fucking matter? Give me some pants. I need to go after her."

Getting to his feet, Brody noted that at least someone had removed the remaining darts from his ass. Travis rummaged through the store shelves and tossed some track pants at him, along with a pink sweatshirt that said, *I support breasts.* The hands cupping the hearts over each pec was a nice touch that earned the younger male a glare.

"It's for a good cause," the bear—who would make a nice rug—replied as he tossed some bills on the counter for the owner.

It fit, and Brody wasn't about to have anyone claim he was too chicken to wear it. But it didn't mean he didn't give Travis a growled promise. "I am going to skin you. Alive."

At that Boris grunted. "Get in line. Jan's already called dibs on his mangy fur. And her mother claims she's got a recipe for bear rump roast."

Travis sputtered. "Hey, it's just a shirt. No need to get all cannibal."

"Says the boy with no respect." Brody rose to his full height, attempting a menacing look while sporting his pink upper body wear. It just didn't have the right effect. What he wouldn't give for camos, kick-ass combat boots, and a big fucking knife. Nothing screamed give me respect like the right outfit.

"Kill me and you get to deal with my mother," the cub threatened.

With a shudder—because only the monumentally stupid messed with Betty-Sue and her infamous spoon—Brody turned away. The grizzly cub would get to live another day.

Or not.

It occurred to Brody that Travis might prove useful as cannon fodder if he could catch the miscreants who took Layla. "I need to find the trail of those who escaped."

Boris, with his impeccable crew cut, shook a negative. "No trail to follow. While you were getting your beauty rest, we scouted out the place and pieced together what happened. Whoever the pricks were, they arrived by truck, a Suburban to be exact, and they left the same way."

No scent to follow. Damn. "What road did they take?"

"The one heading northeast into the outer reaches."

Back to their prison? While Brody didn't know the exact location, he had a good idea. Give him a map and he could probably pinpoint it to within a few miles.

"Your truck gassed?" Brody inquired.

"Yeah, with extra tanks in the back."

"What about ammo and weapons?"

At the incredulous look Boris shot him, Brody laughed. "Okay, stupid question. So we're fully equipped to head out?"

"Yup."

"I take it this means we're not waiting for the others?" Travis inquired from a safe distance.

And leave Layla in the clutches of the freak a moment longer? A growl slipped free.

Boris grinned as he cracked his knuckles. "If we catch them first, then that means more fun for us."

"First though, we need to get this fucking thing off. You got any bolt cutters?" Brody tugged at his collar.

"Nice necklace."

"It's a shock collar."

"Even funnier." Travis smirked but he did locate a tool to pry the sucker off.

The onerous weight gone, Brody felt a hell of a lot better and anxious to go. "Come on, cub. Get your ass moving."

"Shotgun," Travis yelled.

Brody snorted. Like hell was he sitting in the back.

He tripped the younger male on the way out the door and took his spot in the front of the truck. Boris slid behind the wheel.

A dusty and disgruntled Travis clambered in the back. "Uncool," he muttered. "It's a good thing Mother taught me to respect my elders."

"Or else?"

"I'd have grizzlied your ass."

At that, both Brody and Boris laughed. Travis might think he was tough, but he didn't have the years of military training they did.

Nor the edge required to deliver the killing blow.

In a sense, given Travis' positive outlook on life, Brody kind of hoped he never had to learn. Some experiences could never be forgotten and changed a man. Not always for the better.

As Boris drove, a moose on a mission, which involved speed, swerving, and grunting, Brody commandeered a smart phone and pulled up a map of the area. It took him a while, but relying on his recollection of terrain they'd crossed and about how far they'd traveled, he thought he had the area for his incarceration with Layla pinpointed. Problem was, not all the roads in that area were marked, so locating the house was almost impossible. Unless one had access to certain databases via a certain techy back in Kodiak Point.

Brody placed a call to Kyle, only to have a young girl's voice answer. "Hi."

"Hi. Um, is Kyle there?"

"Yes."

He waited. The little girl did too, her whispery breath in the receiver letting him know she still listened.

"Um, can I talk to him?"

"Yeah."

"Now?"

"Okay. Kyle!" From low and lispy to yodel.

Brody almost jumped at the abruptness of it.

A guy said, "Who is it, sweetie?"

"A man."

As the phone changed hands, Brody heard Kyle, whom he recalled was living with some broad and her kid, chuckle. "Yo, man. Who is it, and what's up?"

"I love your secretary."

"So do I, and her mom's not too bad," Kyle added.

"I heard that," yelled a woman's voice.

But Kyle didn't seem worried judging by his laughter. "Brody. My man. Good to hear from you. You kind of disappeared on us, and some folks were actually worried. When none of us got a call for bail, we wondered if you got in a spot of trouble. I was actually just combing through the online newsfeeds and police scanners to see if there was mention of a wolf causing trouble."

"Actually, I was guesting in a cell, just not one owned by authorities. The dick whose been fucking with us thought I'd make an awesome sperm donator."

A guffaw from the back of the truck was not unexpected. "And they chose you?"

Even Boris snickered. "Apparently, they never saw your IQ tests."

Brody flicked a certain finger at his buddy. "Those stupid things don't take into account hands-on ability and street smarts. Put me and one of the creators in the middle of a jungle and let's see who walks out alive."

"Touché, brother. So what did they want your junk for? Create a super army of werewolves?"

"Not sure." Only a partial lie. Brody never did understand what exactly the dude wanted from him other than to impregnate Layla. That he wanted to see if he could recreate her power seemed obvious, but for what purpose? A child wouldn't prove of use for many, many years.

"I take it you weren't calling me to ask about the child support laws for unwilling sperm donors. So what did you need?"

"I need you to find me an address." Because now that Brody had a general area, and given the condition of the house, chances were the place where he'd been held prisoner sat abandoned for years. Abandoned meant someone wasn't paying his taxes to the municipality. Which meant the place might have gone into foreclosure, which would make its location public knowledge.

Put that fucking logic on an IQ test!

Barely brighter than a monkey indeed. As Brody explained his logic, he finally got the respect he deserved.

"I love how your mind works," Travis uttered with awe from the backseat. "That is like some CSI, freaking awesome deduction shit, dude."

Awesome if his theory panned out.

Problematic when his criteria pulled up more than one possible address.

In the end, there were three. Three possibilities. Three chances to fuck up. Brody need to choose one.

Closing his eyes, he let his gut, the instinct that never steered him wrong, choose for him.

But before they could head out, Kyle called them back. Brody answered. "What's up? Did you find another address?"

"I was plotting your cell phone signals to keep track of your location when I noticed an extra blip."

"Blip?"

"I believe you were chipped, dude."

Chipped? Hot fucking damn. That explained how the psycho's minions found him and Layla.

"Where is it?" he growled. "I'll rip the damned thing out myself.

"Good luck with that," Travis replied.

"What's supposed to mean?"

"It means," Travis said as he handed Brody his phone which depicted an enlarged photo of Brody's ass, and the tattoo, "that someone is going to have to play operation on your butt because I'm pretty sure your bunny is only supposed to have two red nipples, not three."

Bare ass in the air while someone of the same sex wielded a knife on his skin?

For that indignity alone, Brody would kill the guy who called himself master. Slowly. Painfully. And if Travis didn't stop laughing, he'd die, too.

Chapter Fourteen

From incredible ecstasy to horror. One moment, Layla was basking in the glow of an intense orgasm, face to face with Brody, who bore an expression so tender she could have sworn he was about to say something. Something momentous. Possibly life changing.

It never passed his lips. In seconds, their door got slammed open, his eyes widened as his body flattened on hers, but only for a moment before his body rolled off and he turned to confront the intruders. It didn't take a genius to figure out what was happening, especially once she felt the familiar sting of the sleeping darts.

The master had found them.

No. Not after this brief taste of happiness. Layla didn't want to go back. She wanted to keep the freedom. Keep the pleasure she'd found in Brody's arms and presence.

She fought the effects of the drug and tapped into her power. It flooded her with sensations; the whispery tingle of minds, some tiny, but others more distinct and aware, signaling a fair-sized animal. If she could bring them to her, perhaps they would provide enough distraction for—

The extra darts hit her, the drugs in them immediately going to work so quickly her eyes couldn't help but slam shut. She was barely conscious when she fell forward, face first into a pillow. Through the lethargy stealing her free will, she thought she heard a howl of rage then nothing.

When next she blinked awake, she had to wonder if escape fifty-seven was but a dream because there above her were familiar bars along with a ceiling she knew all too well.

Was it but a dream?

Even she couldn't imagine that vividly. Her time with Brody wasn't a hallucination. And there were other clues such as the lingering effects of his lovemaking on her body, a soreness between her thighs and a fullness to her well-kissed lips. The scent of him still clung to the shirt they'd dressed her in before carting her back to prison.

A prison that didn't hold him.

As she scrambled to her feet, Layla spun in a circle, seeking him out, searching for a sign he'd returned with her.

Alone.

All alone. What did it mean?

Oh my god did he die during the ambush? Had the master killed her wolf?

The tears that sprang to her eyes surprised her. She'd thought herself past the ability to cry, but it seemed, despite her determination to not care, Brody had snuck past the walls that protected her emotions. He found a spot in the heart she'd thought too jaded to love.

Love?

Could it be? She'd thought it gone for good. Or had it just lain dormant, waiting for the right person? Not just any person. Brody.

The speaker crackled to life, obviously fixed during her flight for freedom. The master's robotic voice boomed. "Welcome back, my pet. I trust your amorous tryst went well."

She didn't reply, huddling on her bed.

"What, nothing to say? How unusual for you. Good thing I am already aware of what happened. I knew you couldn't resist the fellow if given the right opportunity."

"Nothing happened."

"Liar. Or have you forgotten how my men found you?"

How could she forget? "I didn't do it for you." Why the need to justify her actions she couldn't have said, yet it seemed important to state aloud that she'd not slept with Brody to please master, but because she'd wanted him.

"How it happened doesn't matter. The deed is done, and in a few days, we'll know if it came to fruition."

Master and his blasted plan to breed her. "And if it didn't?"

"Is this your subtle way of asking if he's still around for encores?"

"No." But she wouldn't mind knowing if he at least still lived. *Please say he got away or that he is being held elsewhere.*

"Never fear. Your lover lives. Why wouldn't he? The wolf came through for me. Although, he didn't have to be so convincing with his supposed rescue. The men he killed won't be easy to replace."

A cold feeling made her stomach clench. "What are you talking about?"

"Didn't you find your escape too easy?"

Master called the hell they went through to reach safety easy? "We fought every inch of the way."

"To make it seem real, but all along, the wolf was following orders."

"You're lying."

"If it makes you feel better to think so."

"I know so."

"Do you? What do you really know about Brody? Haven't you yet wondered how I found you so easily?"

She'd assumed master had men stationed in nearby towns watching for them to surface. It didn't mean Brody betrayed her. "I know all about your spy network."

"Which I didn't need this time. Not when Brody took you to a predetermined spot."

"I don't believe you." The whole trip wasn't a lie. Brody was as lost as her in those woods. She'd seen him keeping an eye on the sun in the sky as they traveled, making sure they didn't go in circles.

"Did you not find it suspicious none of my men ever actually hit him with bullets? They're not that bad a shot. Come on, Layla, you're a smart girl. Stop denying it. The whole thing was a setup so you'd trust him and let him between your thighs. And it worked."

Robotic voice or not, she could still hear the malicious glee in master's declaration.

She didn't want to believe. Refused to.

No. Not Brody. *Please don't tell me he betrayed me. Not after I let myself trust him. And love him.*

Then again, was she really surprised? History had a tendency of repeating itself.

No. She shook her head to clear it of the insidious thoughts creeping in. Brody was different. If anyone was lying right now, it was master. To what end, she couldn't know.

Or maybe she did.

The master did so enjoy crushing hope and happiness. What better torture could he devise for her than to make her believe the one good thing she'd experienced in her life was a lie?

Master lied.

Brody hadn't betrayed her.

And if he hadn't, if Brody truly did care for her like he'd hinted, then he would come for her, but only if he knew where to find her.

I have to find a way to contact him. Reaching out with her senses, she didn't get far. The thick stone of the basement was still a great barrier to the outside. Within the walls of the house, only the smallest of insects dared survive.

There was nothing she could use.

However, that knowledge didn't frighten her as much as the fact that the master didn't plan to stay.

A pair of guards appeared, one aiming a tranquilizer gun at her. "Cooperate or we'll tag you."

An unfamiliar guard licked his thick lips. "I vote we tag her anyway. Then she won't be able to do a thing about us checking out what she's been hiding under that gown."

"You wouldn't dare." She backed away from them.

The second guard stepped forward, dangling cuffs. "He won't touch you, but only if you behave. On your knees, arms behind your back."

Layla wouldn't win in a battle of strength. Nor could she do anything if they rendered her unconscious. She knelt and laced her hands behind her.

The familiar cold metal restraints almost quashed the remainder of her hope. As they trudged up the stairs though, she tried not to let the remaining tiny flame of optimism extinguish.

Master, dressed in a robe with his usual face mask, awaited them. "Hello, pet. In the mood for a field trip?"

A ball of dread formed in her stomach. "What are you talking about? A trip to where? And why?"

Having met Brody and heard stories of Kodiak Point and its inhabitants, she doubted she could willingly cause them any more harm. Master could threaten all he wanted. She was done trying to hurt people whose only crime was pissing off the psycho who held her prisoner.

"I'm done here. Say goodbye to this blasted country. We're going home."

Home as in back overseas to the dry sands and mountains she'd once come from?

How would Brody ever find her then?

Panicked, she cast out her senses. She needed something that could find Brody. Something she could take over.

There, high overhead, a bird. A lone goose with a small brain, but she didn't need anything more.

She shoved instructions at it but didn't know if they took because a blow to her head sent her staggering to the floor.

"Naughty, pet. Don't you get it? Escape is futile. Don't make me drug you."

"Drug me and you could harm any possible baby."

"Good point. I'm sure Harry over here wouldn't mind knocking you unconscious though if I asked."

Seething behind the hair that had flopped over her face, she muttered. "I'll behave." Until a better chance occurred. She needed to enact escape fifty-eight before she got on the plane. Slim chance of that happening, not with all the men surrounding her and master watching her every move, even if he was a hooded hawk.

What I really need is a miracle.

Chapter Fifteen

I chose wrong. The property Brody let his gut select wasn't the one. He could tell as soon as the long drive ended and the house appeared.

Wrong place. Wrong location. Even worse, time was ticking. A sense of urgency imbued him. *Hurry* his sixth sense screamed. *Hurry, she doesn't have much time.*

Brody jumped out of the truck when Boris stopped and gave the air a sniff, just in case. After all, he'd escaped at night and fought his way free.

A futile hope.

This place belonged to the wildlife that had taken over the house, not a psychopath and his minions.

Angling his head to the sky, he couldn't stop a frustrated howl from bursting free. Frustration gripped him.

Good thing Travis the optimist wasn't affected. "I've got the GPS plotting the quickest route to the next place," he announced from the back of the truck.

"And what if that one is wrong too?" Brody growled. "Fuck." He kicked at the ground in his bare feet, the attire they'd acquired not extending to footwear, not for his size-fourteen feet.

To make his day even fucking brighter, a goose passing overhead chose to drop a hot load, and it spattered his toes.

"You're lucky you're way up there," he yelled to the soaring bird in the sky, "or I'd be roasting your ass for dinner."

As if in answer to his challenge, the snow goose circled down and honked at him before banking away and heading northeast.

"Yeah, you better fly, before I get a gun and shoot." Brody turned and headed back to the truck, only to stop as the goose honked at him again.

It seemed the bird had circled back around, totally atypical behavior even for the aggressive foul. Once more, the goose honked when he saw it had Brody's attention before veering again and heading in the exact same direction as before.

Wait a second… Could it be?

A weapon clicked as a safety was taken off, and Brody had only a moment to knock Boris' arm, sending the shot wild.

"You made me miss!" Boris sounded incredulous, probably because the man was an excellent shot.

"Don't shoot that bird."

"Why the fuck not? He's asking to become dinner."

"Or he's trying to send me a message."

"Have you become completely unhinged?" Boris asked.

"I think that goose is a message from

Layla."

"You think an animal that's best contribution to society is feather pillows and a Sunday cooked dinner—"

"Stuffed with Mom's secret blend of herbs, croutons and bacon, then served with the fluffiest mashed potatoes and fresh biscuits," Travis interjected.

"—is actually some kind of what, secret messenger?" Boris snorted in clear derision.

"And they say I was dropped too many times on my head," said Travis with a laugh.

"I can't explain right now. Just trust me. We need to follow that bird."

"Are you sure?"

"Trust me."

That was good enough for the moose. Problem was, the truck wouldn't make it through the woods.

Brody had to make a split-second decision. It so happened to the northeast was the farthest property they needed to reach—if they took to the roads. However, if a certain nimble wolf went at it on foot?

Shedding his clothes, Brody quickly gave them instructions. "I'll go on four legs. You guys take the road and call in for help. I'll take the cell phone with me. You'll have to harness it so I can carry it in wolf form."

"No problem. I've got something that should work in the back of my truck. Travis, call Kyle and have him put a lock on Brody's signal just in case." Boris added. "Wouldn't want to lose wolfboy again."

"Hardy-har. Look who thinks he's a comedian now," Brody grumbled. "Instead of cracking jokes, why don't you call Reid and the others?" They weren't far behind them at this point, having cut across the state to reach them.

"Yadda, yadda. I know what to do," Boris grumbled. "Just go."

"And save some bad guys for us," Travis added, hanging out the window. "I need to practice my grizzly moves."

Brody couldn't promise anything though, and not just because he'd gone wolf. If anyone dared harm a hair on Layla's head, their lives weren't worth squat. *Hurt my woman and die.*

Reid, Gene, and Boris weren't the only ones who didn't believe in mercy when those they loved were at risk.

Four feet were fleet, especially when on the most important mission of his life. Brody's theory about the goose seemed to hold true, as the avian guide never let him fall too far behind and flew in a straight path through terrain that began to seem familiar.

Was this the ravine he'd jumped in with Layla? He was hopefully on the right side of it. The more he ran, the more sure he became she was close.

He pumped his legs faster, the breeze of his own passage ruffling his fur. He burst from the woods without stopping, relying on surprise. Except there was no one there to greet him.

This was the right place. His nose was sure

of it.

Yet...

The sniper on the roof didn't take a shot because he wasn't there.

The guards patrolling the edge had left signs of their passage in the form of scent and discarded cigarette butts, but none of them raised an alarm.

Even the dogs were gone from the porch.

Despite the ball of dread in his stomach, Brody changed shapes so he could manipulate the door into the house.

Peeling paper. Stained walls. The ugly living room. The dirty kitchen. All of it looked the same as when he'd left. Including the cage in the basement, the one with the door hanging wide open.

His steps slowed at the sight.

Layla wasn't here. Not anymore. He could smell her presence, fresh as if she'd just stepped out, but to go where? Where had they all gone?

Perhaps he'd missed a clue.

Brody returned to the main floor to examine it, but it didn't provide any help.

The upstairs was bare just like Mother Hubbard's cupboard. Layla was gone.

Where has that bastard taken her?

Outside, he hit the garage, only to once again hit a puzzling wall in the form of parked vehicles. If they didn't drive out of here, then where were they? What did that leave?

He needed to slow down and retrace her steps from the house. Except he didn't have to go that far.

There outside, intermixed with at least a dozen other smells, Layla, the psychopath's, all heading in one direction on foot.

Before heading after them, he pulled the phone out of the harness he still wore around his neck. He tapped in a quick message because calling and talking would take too many valuable seconds.

L n L. Short for approach locked and loaded because the area was a hot zone and it was about to get hotter as he heard Layla scream.

Don't worry, sweetheart. The big bad wolf is coming, and he's about to open a can of whoop ass.

Awoo!

Chapter Sixteen

The master had completely lost his mind—not that he had much of one to start with.

The delay on the runway caused by an electrical problem—*thank you, local squirrels, for your timely aid and sharp teeth*—bought Layla time. But once master realized her meddling was the reason for their sitting on the makeshift runway, he drugged her, just enough to dull her senses.

Woozy and bound, she sat on the ground as master paced in front of her, an ominous shape in a billowy black robe. To add insult to injury, he couldn't resist taunting her and confirming her suspicions. "Wait until the wolf realizes you're gone, and that we have his child." The robotic giggle sent a chill up Layla's spine.

"I thought he betrayed me."

"Not intentionally. I was the one who told my men to let you escape. To give you a false sense of freedom so you would feel at ease enough to thank him for your rescue."

"That's sick."

"I prefer the word brilliant. Just like it was my brilliance that planted a tracker in your wolf, which led us right to you."

Hot damn. Well, that explained a lot. Still, though, Layla had questions. "I'm surprised we're leaving so quickly. I mean, all this planning to breed me, what if it failed? I might not be pregnant, in which case all this was a waste."

"Shifters are virile."

"And if I'm not?"

"Then we'll try again. Except next time, maybe we'll rely on science to accomplish the task."

She couldn't help a shudder at the ominous sound of that. "Why are you so determined to see me pregnant?"

"Not just pregnant. Pregnant with *his* child. Of all of them, the wolf is the one who should suffer most for what he's done."

"You know him?"

"In a sense. But enough questions. You're stalling us. Why?" Even though a mask covered the master's features, she could easily imagine a pair of eyes—probably evil red ones like villains sported in paranormal stories—zeroing in on her.

"Maybe I'm just not in the mood to fly."

"Or you're waiting for something? Surely you don't think someone will come to your rescue? The wolf isn't coming for you."

"How do I know you're not lying again?"

"You don't. But it gives me great pleasure to tell you that I know for a fact your lover isn't anywhere close. His GPS tracker hasn't moved from the town we left him in."

"Left him?" Layla snorted. "Say it like it is. Your men faced a little bit of resistance and bolted like the cowards they are."

"No more cowardly than your wolf, who didn't even bother coming after you."

"That's what you think."

Brody's words carried across the open field, and elation filled her.

He came.

"You can't be here. My tracking device shows you miles south of us."

"I fed that little bug to a local rodent."

"You should have stayed away, wolf."

Standing tall—and naked—Brody proved a beautiful sight.

"Leave?" Brody laughed, a low chilling sound that was more mocking than mirthful. "Never. You have something I want."

"You'll never capture me."

"Someone's got a big ego. Who said I was here for you? I'm here for my woman."

Layla had never heard anything sweeter in her life.

"Good luck getting her." The master whirled and barked out orders. "Kill him."

The shifters under the master's command, already converging since Brody's appearance, suddenly raised weapons.

Bad odds. But lucky for Brody, they weren't fast acting.

Within a blink of an eye, Brody had ducked behind an abandoned shipping crate on the edge of the makeshift airfield just in time, as bullets bit the dirt where he'd stood while others pinged into the woods behind him. The thugs continued to fire, their missiles hitting the wooden packing crate, sending splinters flying. Layla could only hope it would provide a thick enough shield to protect Brody.

With the possibility of escape—*here I come number fifty-eight*—Layla tugged at the bonds binding her hands. The drugs in her system hadn't yet dissipated enough for her to use her powers. A shame because if ever there was a time for her to cause a furry stampede, it was now.

It seemed she wasn't to be allowed a chance to escape, or even watch the unfolding drama. Master himself grabbed her by the arm, his thin fingers encased in gloves, bruising her with its punishing grip. He yanked her to her feet.

"Move."

Move toward the plane, which would take her away from Brody?

Not happening.

Layla let her body go limp. The sudden weight broke Master's hold on her, and she hit the ground with an "Oomph."

"Get up and move, I said," barked master, his robotic voice uniform in tenor yet still conveying irritation.

"You'll have to drag me because I'm not going anywhere with you."

Giving someone a method to kidnap wasn't the brightest thing Layla had ever done because master took her literally. Grabbing her by the arm once again, he began to tug her in the direction of the plane, whose engines rumbled to life.

Unable to fight or resist with her bound

limbs, Layla could only watch, and curse, as she saw her chance for escape receding.

Poor Brody was pinned in place by the firepower of master's minions. Everything seemed hopeless. Until the first thug fell with a strangled cry. Then another yelled as a red stain blossomed across his chest.

Reinforcements? Could she be so lucky?

As the gunfire stuttered and then resumed, but firing wildly in numerous directions, Layla realized Brody hadn't come alone.

The odds began to shift.

With a snarl, Brody jumped out from behind his sheltering crate.

Master's minions, though, weren't about to declare defeat. With the advent of reinforcements, they took cover themselves and continued to fire at Brody and the woods, where someone with decent aim kept causing damage.

Master redoubled his efforts to move Layla and got her to the steps going up to the plane. She did her best to wiggle and struggle. Master still tugged her up the hard stairs, and then she was lifted as more hands from inside the vehicle grasped her. The pilot and his second hauled her within the cargo plane.

"Go!" yelled master. "Get us out of here."

"What of the others?" asked the pilot.

"Leave them. They are not important."

Master never did give much care to those under him.

"We have to shut the door," the pilot argued.

"I've got the bloody door. Get your ass to the cockpit and move this fucking plane."

The crew did as ordered, and the whine of the engines revved to a higher pitch. It seemed hopeless, but so long as they hadn't left the ground, Layla wasn't giving up the fight.

When the master moved to shut the door, ankles bound by tape or not, Layla swung her legs and tripped him. He hit the floor hard.

"Why, you bitch," he muttered as he rose to his feet. "You're going to pay for that."

"Then I might as well do this," she sassed as he loomed over her.

She fired her legs out again, this time connecting with a kneecap, which caused master to not only stumble back but scream in pain.

With his attention off her for a second, Layla did her best worm wiggle to the still-open door, only to be brought up short by a fist in her hair. The harsh tug brought tears to her eyes and a gasp to her lips.

"Not so fast, pet."

She cried out again as the plane suddenly lurched into motion, sending master reeling to the side, her along with him, the strands of her hair caught in his fist pulling and, judging by the painful pings, ripping from the roots.

A howl managed to make itself heard over the rumble of the engines. Brody had noticed their imminent departure.

Rapping her chin off the floor, master let go of Layla and made his way to the open door streaming air. As he hauled on the portal to slide it in place and seal the plane, she couldn't help but pray for the first time in years, a whisper, one word, one plea. "Brody."

Unlike those who'd let her down in the past, he heard her and came for her.

Chapter Seventeen

When Brody hit the airfield, even he had to admit his chances of success seemed bleak. As if he'd let bad odds stop him.

Layla was out there. Bound, frightened, and yet, he saw the spark of hope in her eyes when she saw him.

He wasn't about to let that spark die.

Of course, the hooded asshole and his army couldn't do the smart thing and just hand her over. Nope. They wanted a fight. Which he could handle. Problem was they had weapons.

How unsporting bringing guns to a shifter fight.

If those standing against them would have morphed into their animal shapes, he would have totally charged them. Barking seals and even the tusked walrus and nasty looking bison didn't stand much of a chance against a mighty timber wolf.

But no. These guys cheated and brought out the guns, which meant Brody could either die needlessly, a pincushion for bullets, or take cover and hope they either A) ran out of ammo, or B) a fucking miracle occurred, say like he became suddenly bulletproof or the master dude had a change of heart and hopped on his plane minus

Layla.

Or there was option C) which was reinforcements arriving in the nick of time with guns of their own. And not just guns, Boris wielding a gun.

Even better, Boris had the idiot with him. Travis wasn't a good shot, but given he fired from the opposite side of the airfield, it meant those opposing Brody now had to split their attention.

Time to go furry and tear some assholes into pieces.

Changing shapes took only seconds, jumping out with a mighty snarl, a moment more. But in that time the hooded one had managed to yank Layla onboard the plane.

No. No. No.

Brody couldn't let that plane take off. He might never find Layla again if he did.

He spent too much time internally grumbling, and a bullet whizzed by his flank, digging a furrow, which didn't make him yelp, but totally pissed him off.

Watch the fucking fur.

With a howl meant to make the enemy piss themselves, Brody charged. Lucky him, the one thug staring right at him had his gun jam. Ah, the sweet smell of panic and fear, which went well with that of blood when he ripped into the asshole who dared to stand in his way.

Only by chance did another bullet narrowly avoid him, probably because Travis had joined the fray, his massive grizzly shape roaring as he swung his paws, tipped with deadly claws, at anything that moved.

Not exactly a show of finesse, but Travis' enthusiastic swipes did cause damage.

From the sidelines, firing calm as could be, Boris shouted instructions to the cub. "Don't waste your time playing with them. Take the prick out and move on to the next."

The big bear gave a nod then in a much-too-human maneuver punched the man in front of him, which while not exactly in the grizzly bear handbook of fighting technique, did the job.

More important things than analyzing Travis' technique mattered at the moment. Brody had a plane to catch, one that was moving away from him.

Oh, no you don't.

He bolted after it, a cry of pain from Layla spurring him to match the speed of the bouncing plane. As he paralleled it, he leaped into the open portal and his fingers scrabbled to hold onto the edge.

Not exactly a stable spot, but he didn't care, because there was his enemy.

The hooded bastard who'd thought to take him prisoner.

The asshole who'd tortured Layla for so long.

You and I have a score to settle, jerk-off.

Without thought, but lots of pent-up anger, Brody pounced and hit the robed figure, taking him to the floor of the plane.

The figure was slighter than expected, but that didn't stem Brody's rage. Brody snarled and snapped at the covered face, his deadly attack held back by gloved hands.

However he was stronger, and his teeth grew near and nearer…

The plane hit a bump, and he was thrown sideways.

The hooded one took the opening and slithered in the opposite direction. "You should have stayed away," spat the hooded one, the tinny voice crackling, the speaker he used having suffered damage during their scuffle.

Brody shifted so he could reply. "And miss all the fun?" He didn't have time to play games. He needed to end this quickly before the plane left the ground and made things more precarious. He dove for the gun on the floor, only to have a scaled tail whip it away.

What. The. Fuck.

Brody had seen some freaky shit in his life, especially when he served overseas and spent those months in that prisoner camp. However the sight of a man, creature, or whatever still wearing its robe and waving arms while sitting atop a large, coiled serpentine body with a nasty rattle on the end, yeah, that wasn't good news.

He whispered one word. A word that conjured dread—and awakened old fears. "Naga." One of the rarest shapeshifters. Never seen, or at least recorded as being on the North American continent.

So rare actually that Brody knew of only one in existence, and he'd killed it years ago in his escape from the prison. He'd chopped off its head himself before setting fire to the fucker's tent.

I killed you. Killed him but still sometimes heard the sibilant whispers of his dead captor in his dreams.

Just knowing he faced another sent a chill through him. Of all the shifters, the naga was one of the deadliest.

Forget confronting it with just a puny gun. He needed a sword, an army, even better a grenade or a nuke. The bastards were hard to kill and fucking dangerous, especially if it removed its head covering and voice modulator. Nagas didn't just possess uncanny almost bulletproof scales and a poisonous bite. When they spoke, they had the power to hypnotize and compel. Not good.

Time to leave.

It took Brody only a few steps to reach Layla and scoop her. A few more to get to the door.

And only a second to realize the ground was at least eight feet below him and receding.

He held Layla cradled in his arms, and hesitated. He couldn't toss her out. She'd break on impact. If he jumped with her, could he cradle her fall?

"Drop the girl." The sibilant command was rusty and broken, not at all smooth like the last naga he'd encountered, but it still made his arms tremble as he fought to not obey.

"I said drop the girl."

Strain as he might, Brody couldn't fight the order. Even without looking at the naga, it vibrated through him, demanded he obey. So he did. He let go, the disbelief in her eyes as she plummeted piercing him.

Trust me.

Though he didn't speak the words aloud, he hoped she knew enough to read the message in his gaze. Without her to worry about, he could better fight.

He whirled before seeing her land and faced the monster. It still wore a hood and most of its cloak, but the voice modulator hung from ripped wires around its neck. Oh, and while not as big as the last snake shifter he'd encountered, the psycho still possessed enough tail to coil under its upper body. A distorted rattle crowned the tip of its tail and shook with a sound he'd hoped to never hear again.

"Idiot shifter," it hissed. "I wanted the girl."

"And I told you, she's mine. You aren't getting her back."

"Oh, I shall, and I'll keep you. A pair of pets for my new menagerie."

"Like fuck. Burn in hell, asshole." Before his brain could dissuade him from his crazy plan, Brody let himself fall through the open door. As he did, he brought the gun he'd grabbed to bear in front of him. He fired at an engine.

And missed.

"No!" he yelled.

Thankfully, Boris, with two feet firmly planted on the ground, didn't miss.

Boom!

Flames licked from the engine, and it sputtered. Coughed. Whined. But the plane didn't spiral to the ground, even if it didn't sound all too happy.

Speaking of happy, Brody closed his eyes as he prepared to meet the ground.

Instead something soft and squishy broke his fall.

Chapter Eighteen

Seeing Brody plummeting to the ground almost stopped her racing heart. As soon as he hit, miraculously without crushing every bone in his body due to his soft landing, Layla rushed over.

"Are you all right?" she asked, bending over.

Peeking at her with one eye, Brody groaned in reply. "I don't know. You tell me."

"I wasn't talking to you," she replied. "I meant the poor bear under you that broke your fall."

As she'd plunged to the ground, too shocked to scream when Brody dropped her, she'd thought for sure she'd crack her head open like an egg. Instead, a giant teddy of a bear caught her. That same bear also broke Brody's fall.

As he rolled off the poor bear, Brody grimaced. "Thanks for your sympathy."

The furry mound under him stirred and got to its four feet. Relieved her shaggy savior seemed intact, she managed a laugh at Brody's sarcasm. "Anyone who jumps out of a plane isn't looking for sympathy."

"How about thanks?"

"For what? Tossing me out of a plane?"

"But I saved you."

"Yes and so did the poor guy you squashed."

A snort shook Brody. "Poor guy? Bah. That's just Travis."

Just Travis groaned as he shifted from grizzly cushion to man. "Thanks, dude. Next time I won't break your fall. You weigh a ton."

"Do not. But Boris does."

"Boris what?" asked the only dressed male left alive on the field. Toting a gun, he arrived by their side and frowned down at Travis. "Why are you lying on the ground?"

"Because Brody tried to flatten me like a bug."

"Not his fault you couldn't catch him like you caught the girl."

"Yeah," Brody agreed.

The younger male shot them both a dirty look. "Next time, maybe I'll let Boris catch you with his antlers."

"Maybe next time you should," Brody agreed.

"I can guarantee I wouldn't moan about it," Boris added. "My rack is more than up to the challenge of catching a puny wolf."

"Hey!"

Before Brody could protest further Travis interrupted. "I wasn't moaning. I was bitching. There's a difference."

"Neither of which is manly. How am I supposed to toughen you up, boy, if you don't listen?"

"I was listening. Didn't you see me tear off that one guy's arm and use it to smack his buddy?"

"Okay, that wasn't bad, but what about the one who crawled away?"

Their voices trailed off as they strode away from them, the dressed one nudging corpses with his boots while the younger naked one limped alongside gesticulating.

"Friends of yours?" Layla asked.

"Unfortunately," Brody said with a sigh. "You'll have to get used to them. No matter where I go, they seem to follow."

"And why would I get used to them?"

"Well, for one thing, you're free."

"What makes you so sure? Master got—"

A rumble shook the ground as a loud boom echoed over the land. In the distance, black smoke billowed.

A grin crossed Brody's face. "Take that, you fucking snake. As I was saying, you're free of that bastard, which means we can go home to Kodiak Point."

"Who says I'm going there? I mean if I'm free, can't I go anywhere I like?"

He frowned. "No."

"What do you mean no? Do you still not trust me?"

"Oh, I trust you. I mean no as in you're not going anywhere without me."

"And why is that? Am I your prisoner?" She wanted to hear him say it. To say he wanted her with him.

He didn't let her down.

"More like I'm yours. You did more than capture me that night by the rock. You stole my heart, Bait."

"You know I hate that name." She tried not to let the flutter of excitement at his words make her do something silly, like declare undying love, the knowledge she loved him still too new and frightening.

"I know you hate it, *Bait*, but if you're going to make me pay for it, I guess you'll have to stick around."

"To punish you of course."

"But of course. Naked, too, you know, so we don't ruin perfectly good clothes. Maybe with some handcuffs for good measure."

A smile curled her lip. "Sounds like torture."

"Definitely. But of the most decadent kind."

Pleasurable, too.

They moved closer to one another until they were but a hairsbreadth apart, close enough that she had to tilt her head to watch his face.

"I guess since you're in such need of correction, I could visit your town for a while."

"A long while. I have a feeling I'm going to need lots of punishment. *Bait*." His eyes twinkled with mischief, and she couldn't help but grin wider in response.

And just like that, they were suddenly in each other's arms, kissing and hugging, fanning the flames that never seemed to extinguish when they were together.

In between nibbles, she murmured, "I can't believe you came for me."

"I can't believe you thought I wouldn't."

"And I can't believe you guys are making out in the open like that. Get a fucking room!" shouted Boris.

That unfortunately took longer than expected because the rest of the cavalry arrived in time to admire their handiwork.

Tucked against Brody's side, Layla was treated to a parade of new faces, most of them regarding her with curiosity but none with hostility. They seemed more amused by Brody's reluctance to leave her side and his growl of warning if someone wandered too close or stared too long.

Once it was ascertained the area was clear of the enemy, Layla was properly introduced to Reid, alpha of Kodiak Point.

Dark eyes in an uncompromising face assessed her. "So you're the girl who can talk to the animals."

"Like Dr. Dolittle?" Travis exclaimed.

"Who?" Layla asked.

"Ignore my idiot cousin," Reid replied. "I ran out of duct tape, but if he continues to drive me insane, I'm sure we can find some super glue somewhere."

Travis clamped his lips and managed to look offended.

"Brody says you were a prisoner of the dude who has been fucking with us."

She nodded. "I've been captive in one

shape or another since I was fourteen."

The winces all around were hard to miss, as was the hollered, "Hey, Gene, you no longer hold the record for longest prisoner of a sadist."

"I didn't realize it was a competition," replied a guy with shocking white hair, brilliant blue eyes, and a scar that bisected his face.

"I'd gladly give you the title," she added with a grimace.

"How about instead we rid you of the reminder of your incarceration?" Reid offered. "Someone grab some bolt cutters, and let's get this collar off her."

The snap as the ring cracked off was a welcome sound, but not as welcome as the lightness once the physical symbol of her life as a prisoner was removed.

She touched her fingertips to her neck. "Is it truly over?"

"You're free now, sweetheart." Brody's husky murmur went well with the one-armed hug he gave her.

Free? How she liked the sound of that.

"Yes, you are free," Reid confirmed. "But I do hope you'll consider sticking around for a while. Even if the dude behind the attacks on our clan is gone, we have questions. We've got more than enough room for you in our town, and a support system to help get you on your feet."

It sounded like more than she deserved, but she couldn't help a spurt of guilt. "It's a nice offer, but will your town accept me after everything I've done?"

"They forgave me, even though I was a real prick," the one called Gene said.

"Still is a big prick," Brody confided in a low whisper.

"I heard that, wolf."

"Good to know that mating hasn't completely ruined you," Travis snickered. Then ducked as Gene shot out a fist, which only barely missed the younger man.

"Ignore them," Reid said with a forbearing expression. "I do. But the offer is genuine. Come to Kodiak Point. See if you like it. We could always use someone with your talent on our side."

Antics aside, the offer of acceptance blew her away. They were offering a chance to atone, to belong. A chance for a true home and maybe more.

If I'm not imagining things, I do believe Brody is hinting at something permanent. She peeked at Brody and found reassurance in his warm gaze.

"I think I'd like that."

"Then it's settled. Travis, why don't you drive them back to Kodiak Point? I think they've had enough excitement for the moment. We can always talk when I get back. The rest of us will examine the house and surrounding area. I am hoping we'll find some clues about the prick who was in charge."

"You sure?" Brody asked.

"Yeah, but if you'd like to argue about it, I might just find reasons to keep my beta here."

"I wasn't asking if you were sure about me leaving but more about putting me in a vehicle with your dumbass cousin for several hours. What if I'm tempted to kill him?"

Reid snorted. "As if you'd piss off his mother. She might stop making you those ridiculous Shaggy and Scooby Doo-sized sandwiches if you do."

"And pie. I mustn't do anything to ruin my chances for pie," Brody added. "Come on, Bait. Let's blow this joint before they find jobs for us."

The ride to Kodiak Point was more than a few hours, but luckily they stopped just three hours in at a small hamlet that sat alongside a gorgeous lake. There was a hunting lodge on the edge with empty rooms, which they rented for the night.

Brody ensured they got an end unit, far from everyone, especially Travis, who never shut up. But Layla enjoyed his rascally chatter as his non-stop stream painted a picture of not only Brody but the town he was taking her to.

As Brody ushered her to their room, she couldn't help but ask, "Is it true you single-handedly saved most of the men I just met?"

"They would have done the same for me. You're not the only one who spent time behind bars, prisoner of a sadist."

Just one more thing she had in common with him and those who seemed so ready to accept her in their fold. "I still can't believe I'm free."

"Believe it. And enjoy it. We should celebrate."

"Really? How?"

He waggled his brows.

She giggled. "That isn't sexy you know."

"Oh, yes it is."

"Says who?"

"Me. Because, despite your claim, you're about to get naked for me and we're going to indulge in wild, passionate sex."

"Is that an order?"

"No, it's a promise."

That wasn't the only promise they exchanged that night.

After a steamy shower, and not just because of the hot water, they tumbled into a bed, a real big one with clean sheets and a fluffy comforter.

But no pajamas.

She shivered with delight, not cold, his body covering hers, the skin-to-skin contact scorching.

"So when are you going to admit it?" he asked in between kisses.

"Admit what?"

"That you love me."

"Do not."

"Liar."

"Why don't you say it first?" she countered.

"Oh ho, challenging me, are you? Fine. I'm not a coward. I love you, Bait. I think I have since that first freaky moment when I saw you sitting on that rock like some sort of animal-whispering goddess."

"And I think I fell in love with you when I saw your floppy pink bunny."

"Um, Johnson is not too crazy about you referring to him as floppy."

"I wasn't talking about that part of your body. I fell in love with your ass."

"Really?" Brody craned to peer over his shoulder. "It wasn't my charm?"

"You weren't initially very charming."

"My hair?"

"Is in need of a major trim."

He growled. "Woman, my hair is perfect, and you know it."

Layla laughed. "Okay, I'll admit I like it especially since it's long enough to do this." She gripped his wild locks and drew him down for a kiss. Then another.

In no time at all their breathing came in shallow bursts, their tongues were hopelessly entwined, and he was grinding against her.

When he said, "Roll over," it took her a moment to filter his command.

"Why?"

"Because we're going to try something new, unless you're chicken…" He purred the words against her earlobe before tugging it with his teeth.

A new experience? Layla didn't need to be asked twice. She hungered for new. Needed to experience and try everything she'd been denied for so long.

Onto her stomach she flipped. She gasped as he drew her hips upward, positioning her so her buttocks rose in the air, exposing her to his gaze.

It should have embarrassed her, but this was Brody, Brody who murmured almost reverently, "You are so bloody perfect, sweetheart. And mine."

His possessive words made her sex clench and moisten. How she wanted him, needed him, and yet he seemed content to toy with her, rubbing the head of his shaft against her moist core. She peered over her shoulder, a come-hither glance she hoped conveyed her fervent need. It proved all the invitation he needed.

Wrapping an arm around her waist, he anchored her before he nudged deeper into her wet slit with the tip of his rod. A shudder rocked her as anticipation almost boiled over. She might have commended his attempt to take it slow as he eased himself into her tight channel, but Layla was too aroused for such a measured pace. She rocked back against him and sheathed him deep.

Her wolf threw his head back and emitted a short howl. "Mine," he growled. "My woman. My mate."

"Yes, yours," she whispered. But his because she wanted to belong to him. Because she *chose.*

It seemed he liked her reply because he slammed into her willing flesh, fast and hard. Layla clawed at the sheets and moaned with utter abandon. Each thrust drew forth a cry. Each pump struck a sensitive spot inside. Each time he pounded in, she drew closer and closer to the edge.

His body curved over hers, cradling and heating. His lips caressed the top of her shoulder as he continued to thrust, and when she finally came, her sex convulsing around his pulsing shaft, he bit her. Not a gentle nibble, but a firm chomp that broke skin.

She might have protested, except it launched her into a second orgasm, one more powerful than the first, and for a moment, just a moment, their minds touched and she could see his love for her. See it. Feel it. Know it.

It was the most intense moment of her life.

The start of her new, free life.

A life with no more torture or fear or cages. Only love.

And ice cream, which he fetched for her, along with chocolate sauce. Damn was that stuff good on everything. And she meant *everything*.

Epilogue

"We only found two bodies in the plane wreckage." Reid's stark announcement hung in the air of the meeting room—also known as Reid's garage, where Brody, the other boys and their clan doctor—also known as their voice of reason—had gathered to discuss recent events.

"Two? Not three?" Brody frowned.

"Any idea who they were?" Boris asked.

"One was definitely human, the other some kind of avian shifter."

But no snake. Not in the wreckage, nor in the environs. The one who called himself master still lived. And so long as he did, they weren't safe. *Layla is in danger.*

Fuck.

Totally unacceptable.

Brody wasn't the only one to come to that conclusion.

Gene drummed his fingers on the armrest of his seat. "We should mount up a hunting expedition. Now that we know we're looking for a reptile shifter, maybe we'll be able to find a trail."

"We already did. It seems our *friend* somehow managed to escape the crash unscathed."

"And you know this how?" Brody asked.

Kyle spoke up. "My contacts in the city reported that an aircraft was hijacked midflight and redirected."

"What makes you think it's our dude?"

"No one remembers what he looked like. And guess where the plane landed?"

Overseas. Back to the land where the desert gobbled land, sand wedged itself in tender places, and war still waged. A war they thought they'd left behind.

"What do we do?" In other words, should they remain tucked in their haven on the other side of the ocean or—

Reid stood, and his eyes sparked. "Fuck waiting to see if the bastard comes back. I say we get our asses over there and show him why you don't screw with our fucking clan."

All in favor?

Unanimous.

More details were hammered out, but they didn't waste a ton of time on them. The flight was a long one, which meant plenty of time to plan. Besides, the naga already had a head start. Before it could find reinforcements, they needed to catch up and end his life once and for all. End it before he could try and take Layla back.

The meeting broke up, with the guys and the doc heading off to pack.

Brody dreaded breaking the news to Layla.

How do I tell her that psychopath is still on the loose?

As he pulled into the driveway of his place,

he noted the geese perched on the roof, keeping watch—and shitting on the shingles. Pesky birds. It drove his neighbors nuts that they couldn't eat them.

Other signs his life had changed?

The grass didn't need mowing. It hadn't since he'd brought Layla home, the wild goats she'd adopted doing the job for him.

Brody barely batted an eye when he walked into the house and found a hedgehog rolling on the shag carpet in the living room, fluffing the strands.

He didn't flinch when he heard the hum of bees in the pantry, making honey. Honey Reid kept his paws off, given Layla's stinging rebuke—administered by said bees.

Brody, however, drew the line at any pets in the bedroom—it took only one set of big kitty cat eyes staring, and judging his technique, for him to ban her nighttime foot warmer permanently.

As he trekked through the house, he noted all the places she wasn't. His mate wasn't in the bedroom or the empty kitchen. Nope. Not his special lady.

Forget cooking and cleaning. His sweetheart didn't have the knack or patience for those. Instead, he found Layla out in the backyard, practicing knife throwing.

What a beautiful sight she made, her long hair loose and her expression intent. Slim fingers wrapped around the hilt of the sharp dagger he'd given her—and he knew well that grip. At least his cock did, and it hardened in remembrance.

She whipped the blade, just like he'd taught her, and nicked the edge of the bull's-eye. Nice shot. Not that he said it aloud, not in his mischievous mood.

"If it isn't my domestic goddess hard at work keeping the house tidy and her man happy."

He ducked just in time and only lost a few strands of hair.

No, not the hair!

She knew how he loved his furry locks. But he didn't get an apology.

"What have I told you about sneaking up on me?" she huffed, hands on her hips.

"What have I told you about drafting the wildlife to do chores?"

She wrinkled her nose. "I know. It's immoral. It freaks folks out and all the rest. But, Brody, I have to. I suck at cleaning and cooking and all that other stuff the women do."

"You don't suck at it." Actually, she did. Layla wasn't June Cleaver when it came to housekeeping. "You hate chores. There's a difference."

The pout on her lips was utterly adorable. "Why can't I have a more exciting job? And don't you dare suggest I go work at the diner or the store again. You know I hate being cooped inside and serving people." A flurry of knives went flying as she drew and flung them rapid-fire at the target. She'd learned a lot the last two weeks. Enough that she deserved a break from domestic hell.

"I know you hate the idea of a regular job almost as much as housework, which is why you and I are going on a trip."

This time he sidestepped the missile, which barely missed his ear.

"Oops. Sorry about that. You took me by surprise because I thought I heard you say something about a trip."

"I did."

"Where to? Not that Walmart the next town over. I thought we were banned."

He grinned as he recalled that excursion. When Layla had said it wasn't fair only children got to ride in the carts, he took her for a jog through the store with her giggling madly—until management kicked them out. He shook his head. "Nope. We're going farther than that. Like over-an-ocean far."

Her eyes narrowed. "What happened to staying in Kodiak Point where it's safe? Keeping me out of temptation's path and all that blah, blah, blah."

"The blah blah blah part is why we're going. I think it's time we both admitted it. We're not cut out for the domestic life. You want adventure. I want adventure. There's an evil villain still at large that needs capturing."

"Excuse me? Rewind. What evil villain?"

"So it turns out our snake friend isn't quite dead. But don't panic. He's also not on this continent anymore."

"Where is he then?"

"Overseas, somewhere. Which is where the travel part comes in. Reid is mounting a strike force to go after him. What do you say we go with the others and find him?"

"You want me to go with you?"

"Why wouldn't I? You've proven you can take care of yourself." And he'd be by her side if she faltered. "You know the land. You know what to expect. I can't think of a better partner than you. That is if you want to go?"

If she'd had shifter strength, she might have crushed him with her enthusiastic yes.

In between rib crushing she asked, "We're going to my homeland?"

"Yes. Me, you, Boris, Travis, if his mother lets him, and a few others."

"You aren't afraid the master will recapture me?"

"Let him try. We're together now, which means if he messes with you, he messes with me."

"I like the sound of that. However I'd prefer the sound of him screaming as we take care of him once and for all." Her evil smile held a hint of bloodthirsty that he loved.

"You say the sexiest things," Brody growled. "I love you, Bait."

"And I love you, Thud."

While he could have done without his nickname, he never got tired of hearing her say she loved him and, even better, knowing she trusted him. They might have started out their relationship both expecting the worst, but it turned out his capture was the best thing to ever happen to him.

Who would have thought a wolf's capture would lead to rapture?

*

"I'm going and that's final, Ma." Travis finished shoveling clothes in his duffel bag, ignoring his mother and her wooden spoon, which wasn't easy. Instinct screamed to not turn his back lest she tan his hide.

But he was a man now, not a cub. And, as a man, it was time he cut the apron strings she insisted on keeping, starting with this trip.

More like a mission. A real one. Overseas and everything!

"But who will keep you safe?"

"I can keep myself safe. Not to mention, the other guys are going with me. Brody's coming, along with Boris and Gene." Poor Reid couldn't, not with so many of the clan already volunteering to go. Someone needed to keep Kodiak Point running. The joys of leadership, something Travis most definitely did not crave. He had his hands full enough trying to keep his mother from running his life.

"But I'll miss you."

He relented a little and hugged the woman who'd raised him. He loved his ma, even if she was violently overprotective and scared all his friends—actually anybody who knew her.

"I'll miss you, too, but it's time for you to let me go."

"Don't you go falling for any of those local girls."

Not likely. Travis already had an eye on a woman, problem was she barely seemed to notice he was alive. But he planned to change that on this trip.

Hold on tight because I intend to show you a grizzly kind of love. Rawr.

The End

The Kodiak Point series concludes with the rascally Travis in Grizzly Love. More info at EveLanglais.com

Made in the USA
Lexington, KY
21 November 2016